REA

Belly Fruit

OTHER BOOKS BY LYNNETTE D'ANNA

sing me no more

RagTimeBone

fool's bells

Belly Fruit

Lynnette D'anna

NEW STAR BOOKS

VANCOUVER

2000

New Star Books Ltd.
107 - 3477 Commercial Street
Vancouver, BC   V5N 4E8
www.NewStarBooks.com

Cover: Steedman Design
Cover photograph: Una Knox
Typeset by New Star Books
Printed & bound in Canada by Transcontinental Printing & Graphics
1 2 3 4 5 04 03 02 01 00

Publication of this work is made possible by grants from the Canada Council, the British Columbia Arts Council, and the Department of Canadian Heritage Book Publishing Industry Development Program.

CANADIAN CATALOGUING IN PUBLICATION DATA

D'anna, Lynnette, 1955–
  Belly fruit

  ISBN 0-921586-79-5

  I. Title.
PS8557.A568B44 2000   C813'.54   C00-910980-3
PR9199.3.D26B44 2000

To all the dispossessed
and for ebf, a mirror.

All art is quite useless.
OSCAR WILDE

precious diva

It may be true that many people in this world are anonymous but when Nancy disappears she leaves a space. George hears it on the radio. *Nancy Rider . . . renowned artist . . . this morning in New York . . . Vancouver-based . . . daughter of . . . Police are searching . . .*

First she calls the CBC to confirm the story, Nancy's number next and then the cops. Dazed and in a dream, she takes the red-eye to New York and when she arrives there is a body to identify. There is no one besides George who belongs to her so she will be the one to clean the flat containing personal effects and the art she has been working on.

The paintings stacked against the walls answer any questions she might have had as to what exactly Nancy has been up to; on these canvases she poured out with utter elegance what she conjured from the life around her and the scars she held inside. Only Nancy could draw brilliance from such torment. She has achieved it, her life's work. *She slept here*, George tells herself. *Lived, ate, drank, fucked and bled with it.*

After emptying her churning belly she summons Nancy's agent Nino. "You had better get these things out of here," she warns. "Right away. Before I do something rash."

A bowling ball, squat and bald, he arrives in minutes. In greeting he takes her hand and lifts it to his mouth. "I am Nino and you are George; I am so pleased you call me soon. Whatever is our precious diva gotten herself into?"

George does not want this one to touch her. She shudders and tugs back her hand. "See for yourself," she tells him curtly.

Peering through thin spectacles he examines each piece at length.

1

Then he stands back and smiles. "This one!" he pronounces happily. "This one, she never disappoints! She has so enormous talent."

"Yes," retorts George angrily. "Yes, she had."

His gesture is expansive. "For Frankfurt. Unfortunately it will be posthumous. I will pack and transport; no damage will be done."

His toothy smile, the gleeful rubbing of his hands with corpse not cold reminds George of Dickens, something from a dim bleak past better left behind. "It killed her," she says loudly.

"Yes, so sad. I will miss our little diva."

"You're not hearing me. I mean this work, it is responsible."

"You intend to mean some lunatic with a knife. It is New York, ridiculous! I agree."

"No! I mean these paintings. You must destroy them. They should not be shown."

He bristles. "She intend these for Germany, it is in our contract. Legal, completely. Some psycho with a blade will not arrest this talent. Nor will you."

"These people posed for her; they were part of her life. The paintings might contain important clues. Maybe the cops will want to see them. They might help identify her killer."

Nino waves his arms wildly. "No, no! I will dispose. Everything must go through me!" He scampers, gathering evidence in his greedy arms. "No cops! I have full contract, legal. I take now, immediately. Downstairs there is a truck."

She doesn't want to leave this vulture alone with Nancy's things, but neither can she bear to stay and watch him add it up, can't bear to hear him calculating Nancy's life in terms of cents and dollars. How well she knows there is absolutely nothing she can do to stop the machinery of what will happen next. "I have to get some air," she says.

"Not to worry little one," he soothes, relieved. "I have revered our diva. I will take the utmost caution, I assure."

George slinks down hopeless sidewalks, stepping over broken bodies wherever they have fallen from perversity, exhaustion or poverty. Nancy liked the defeated exhibited like this, out here in the open for all the world to see. She said that it was honest. Now George will pack up her possessions and arrange for their transport back to Canada. When she returns to Nancy's flat, Nino will be gone and she will call Jean Paul. He should be back from Edmonton by now and she needs to hear his voice.

transit

The woman plowing down the aisle of the Greyhound with too many bags chooses Zoey to sit beside. She spreads her things all around herself while Zoey stares through the window to the spot she last saw Eli.

"How far you going?" asks the woman.

Zoey swallows. "To the coast."

"How long will you be on the road?"

"A couple of days, I guess."

"Going out to visit family?"

"Nope."

"Friends?"

Zoey shifts. "Oh, you brought a pillow. I never even thought of doing that."

"You should always bring a pillow. And a blanket. When they turn on the air conditioner, it gets mighty cold. I always take the bus to see my daughter and her kids in Saskatchewan." Zoey reaches into her pack and tugs out Eli's farewell gift. Rapidly she flips pages while her seatmate watches. "You like to read?"

"Yeah."

"Same here. But I never had much patience for poetry. I don't understand it. You know Danielle Steel?"

"I don't have patience for that kind of writing," says Zoey. "There's way too many words."

"Nothing I like better'n a good love story."

"There's no such thing."

"What's the matter, sweetie?" The stranger clucks. "You don't believe in love?"

"I believe in it all right. I just don't think it's ever any good."

The woman crosses her arms. "You're still young. Someday you'll find the right man and then you'll sing a different tune, you mark my words."

Zoey smiles politely and turns her attention to the book. To Eli's inscription on the inside leaf. *for Zoey with love.* But as usual he didn't sign his name.

When she awakens, her seat-mate has gone. All across the Prairies, day and night to dawn in Calgary and then the foothills. Through the Rockies, cliffs and streams just like a dream. Her stomach knots and boils, it's hard to breathe but it has nothing to do with mountains and chasms. The cord she's stretching from is thinning; what she has left behind is home, lover, mother, baby.

When she was twelve she took this trip on VIA with her mother. In the observation car she met a man who rubbed his sweaty palms along the inside of her thighs and with thick breath asked her how she liked the train. "I like it fine," she said trying to ignore his creeping hands. Shuffled her feet, clamped tight her knees while he chattered on and on. Finally she saw her mother navigating down the aisle around knees and elbows, searching for her child. She arrived at last and that was the end of that.

When she gets off the bus in Vancouver her legs are stiff and she is shivering. She lights a cigarette and hails a cab.

"No smoking," says the cabbie but he waits for her to finish.

"Can you take me to a bed-and-breakfast near one of the beaches?"

"Sure thing. Where you from?"

"Manitoba."

"You here to see your family?"

"I don't have a family."

"Left 'em all back east?"

"I said I haven't got a family."

"Seems like everybody in this place is on the run from something. I guess if you go as far as you can go, you end up here. We got more wanted criminals per capita than we know what to do with. The other provinces don't want 'em back so they get to stay." While he manipulates the cab he crunches peanuts, dropping shells like Hansel through his open window.

Although Zoey is not a wanted criminal she has also gone as far as she can go, to the very edge of Canada where the air hangs heavy with the balmy scent of rain and roses. The first place he stops has a vacancy. The manager takes her money and gives her keys. "This one's for your room," she points. "This one's for the bath and this is for the entry. Breakfast is at seven; if you miss that you're on your own. No meals, music, visitors or smoking in your room. There's a pay phone on every floor. You come by bus or train?"

"Bus."

"Nice way to travel, you get to see the mountains. How long you plan to stay?"

"I'm not sure yet."

"If you pay on time and follow the rules, you can stay forever if you want."

The room is small but clean and near the water so there is a view. After a hot shower she binds herself in thick clean cotton and races back along the hallway to her room where she quickly shuts and locks the door. From her pack she tugs a baggy tee, one of Eli's borrowed months ago to stretch around her growing belly, slides it over her head and sinks into the borrowed bed despite the nagging beauty of a steaming sunset. Surrounded by a lullaby of strange house sounds, she falls asleep.

She awakens on Manitoba time, which means she can get breakfast if she wants it. Thinks of calling Eli but he might not be at the office yet and she doesn't want to leave a message for his new receptionist to hear. She takes the city map from the bureau so she won't get lost; buys latte and bagel on the way. At the beach she tugs off her sandals and settles on a log.

While coastal sunlight marks her skin, Zoey sprints a rusty railroad ladder laid across the prairie. Heel-over-toe, heel-over-toe. Earth stretched flat as far as she can see. Whistle cracks a warning and she leaps to safety in the nick of time. *This must be a good omen*, she remembers thinking. *That train could have crushed me.*

wanted

George sticks the *help wanted* sign she drew up last night on the outside door of the theatre where Zoey spots it during her post-beach ramble. "How can I apply?" she asks.

George rolls the masking tape onto her wrist like a bracelet. "I wasn't expecting anyone so soon. But I guess there's no reason we can't talk now. Come with me." She leads the girl inside, eyeing her while waving her into a chair overloaded with programs, posters, fax and computer print-outs. Shoulder-cropped copper hair, moist green eyes, energetic, slender and petite. George laughs. "Grab a seat if you can find one."

Zoey gathers up an armful of the clutter, sets it carefully on the floor and sits. "I'm Zoey." She thrusts her hand across the desk.

Greedily George clasps it feeling skin, soft, smooth and warm. "My name is George. I'm the general manager of this place."

"Did you say Georgia?"

"No, just George. My mother wanted me to be an artist. It was a toss-up between Georgia for O'Keeffe and George for Sand."

"Is that why you ended up in a theatre? Because of your mother?"

"I'm not really in the theatre; this job just pays my rent. I'm a writer in my other life." George pauses, realising she is still grasping Zoey's hand. She releases it and leans back in her chair. "So. Tell me about yourself. You're not from here, are you?"

Zoey picks at her sleeve with her discarded hand. "I'm not sure what you're looking for but I can type, answer phones, take messages, I'm super-organised and I learn quickly."

"Have you ever worked full-time before?"

9

"Of course I have! I was office manager for an architecture firm in Manitoba for the past two years. I just quit."

"Why?"

"This seemed as good a time as any. I wanted to travel for awhile. You know, see different places and meet new people. I've lived in Roseville practically my whole life."

"Could you supply a reference or two?"

"You can talk to my ex-boss if you want." Zoey rests her elbows on the metal arms of the chair, crosses and uncrosses her ankles. "I can tell you think I'm younger than I am, everybody always does. It's because I'm short. But I'm almost twenty." She reaches for her bag. "I have ID if you want to see it."

George waves her hand. "It isn't necessary; I believe you. What I'm looking for is someone to deal with the garbage that's accumulated here. I never have the time to organise so it all piles up, as you can see. And managing the box office once the season gets underway in fall. You think you could handle that?"

"Sure."

"When could you start?"

"Right this minute if you want."

"Not so fast! I barely put up the sign. And I still have to talk to your ex-employer."

"It's long-distance."

"That's not a problem."

"Okay, I'll write down his number for you. Have you got a pen?" George slides a pad of paper and a pen across the desk and Zoey scribbles down a name and number. "Should I check in with you later on today? Or sometime tomorrow?"

"I could call you."

"I don't have a phone. I'm staying at this bed-and-breakfast."

"Then why don't you call me? Here's my card. Around ten?"

"Sure thing." Zoey releases her sneakers from the chair rungs, stands and leans across the desk, passing George her fingertips. "Thanks," she says. "I really hope I get this job."

"I appreciate your stopping by," says George. "We'll talk tomorrow. Don't forget to call."

Once outside the theatre, Zoey quickly finds a pay phone. "Collect," she tells the automated operator.

Eli answers on the first ring. "Froese and Thatcher," he says stiffly.

"You have a collect call from Zoey. Press one to accept the charges . . ." There's a beep and then he shouts, "Zoey! Where the hell are you?"

She clutches the receiver tightly. "Eli, listen . . ."

"Where are you? I can barely hear you! Are you coming home?"

She clears her throat. "Eli, listen! I'm at a pay phone outside and it's really loud. There's this woman, her name is George, she'll be calling for a reference. It's about a job."

"Why are you looking for a job?"

"I have to do something. Can you hear me?"

"You weren't supposed to be settling down out there! The plan was for you to take a little holiday and come right back. Now all of a sudden I hear you're looking for a job."

"I can't explain right now. Just give me a reference, okay? Pretty please? She's probably trying to get through to you this minute. We're tying up the phone."

"What kind of job is this?"

"It's in a theatre, you know, with a stage for plays and stuff. She wants me to do the box office, cleaning up and filing . . . Please be sweet; don't embarrass me."

"You don't need the money Zoey," says Eli tersely.

"I can't hear you, El. There's a bus beside me. I'm gonna hang up now, okay?"

"You don't need a job!" he yells. "Zoey, wait! How can I get a hold of you?"

The line is busy the first time George tries the number but the second time it's answered by a man who identifies himself as Elijah. "I'm calling about Zoey," she tells him. "She named you as a work reference."

"Zoey."

"Yes. She said she was your office manager. What can you tell me about her?"

"She ran this office. What else do you need to know?"

"Were there problems with her work?"

"No! No, of course not! No problems, she's a great worker. But the truth is . . ." He pauses. "Well, the truth is I'd prefer it if you didn't hire her. She's supposed to be coming back; that was my understanding of it. And besides, it's utterly ridiculous to ask me for a reference. Zoey is much more to me than office help."

"Excuse me?"

Eli clears his throat. "To be perfectly frank," he says softly, "Zoey is my lover. So there is no way I can be objective. I just want her to come home. Please get her to call me; I don't even have her number."

dear Eli

Dear Eli,

Today I was out sight-seeing when I saw this help wanted sign on a theatre door and I thought what the hell, this might be interesting. Like I told you when I phoned, that woman George who runs the place said she was going to get a reference from you. Please don't be mad at me, this is something I have to do. I know I don't need the money but I just can't go back yet. I don't know if I can explain. It's so weird and scary to be away from you. It feels like a part of me is missing, an arm or a leg or something that other people should be able to see. But obviously they can't because nobody has said where's the rest of you or anything like that. But you've got your own life and you don't need me around to mess it up any more than I already have. Anyway I really want this job. And George is a real writer! Maybe I'll get to be friends with her and find out how to get my poems published.

all my love Z.

mistress

The next morning Zoey rings the theatre at precisely ten o'clock. "I read one of your books last night," she says. "So do I get the job?"

"Where did you find my book?" George asks.

"At the bookstore. I think it's beautiful; I loved it. So. Are you giving me the job?"

"It's all yours!"

"Because I said I liked your book?"

George laughs. "It can't hurt. But seriously, I'm flattered that you read my book but I'm giving you the job because I talked to your ex-boss."

"Oh. What did he tell you about me?"

"He said he wants you to call him."

"Is that all?"

"He told me not to hire you. He said that you and he were lovers. Correction, he said *are* not *were*. Therefore he can't be objective and he wants you back."

"Well, now you know it all," says Zoey tightly. "When do I start?"

"Could we meet for lunch?"

"As in today?"

"As in two hours from now."

"Alrighty!" says Zoey. "I'll be there!"

George paces through the empty theatre. The wet dream she awakened with this morning has stirred her up. Something about this girl, she can't quite put her finger on it. She walks the floor like a nervous virgin bride, lifting stacks of paper then setting them back down. Again and again she looks at her watch until at last Zoey appears breathless in the doorway. George checks, same eyes, same hair, same to-die-for body.

14

"I can kill time if I'm too early," she offers. "You want us to meet somewhere?"

"No!" says George too loudly. "No," she repeats more softly. "This is just fine. I've been waiting for you." When their fingers meet on the doorknob she forces herself to let go. "Go ahead," she says, stepping back. "I should lock up."

It's a perfect July day, the sort of day that makes you ache for a lover you haven't met yet. The falafel man gives them extra toppings and paper bags instead of styrofoam containers without being asked.

"He's nice," says Zoey. "Friendly."

"He is when his wife's not there." They reach for the walk button at the same time and when they touch, shivers wipe down George's spine.

The girl chatters on until they reach Kits Beach. There she drops onto a bench and gazes all around without uttering a single word. George removes the sandwiches from her satchel, passes one to Zoey and then quickly fills her mouth. When she is finished eating, she crumples up her wrappings and tucks them in her bag to dispose of later. Then she leans back and clears her throat. "Let me tell you about this job. The Vancouver Community Theatre is a performance space where local artists can stage drama, dance, films, music, have book launches . . . you name it. There's only one show between now and September when the season really starts. Until then I want you to sort stuff, get rid of garbage and update our archives. I'm the general manager. I take care of the business end of things like accounting, bookings, grant applications and dealing with the board."

"So basically you want me to clean up."

"In a nutshell. I know we haven't discussed your salary. We're a non-profit society so we can only pay nine-fifty an hour and any overtime you put in will be earned time off."

Zoey shrugs. "Whatever. It's cool with me. I don't actually need the money."

"May I ask why you want the job then?"

"I need something to keep me busy. If I hang around being a tourist,

I'll probably go back before I'm ready out of sheer boredom."

"In that case," says George, "I'm not sure about giving you this job. I want someone I can count on to stick around for at least awhile. I can't promise you a permanent position, but I don't want to train you just to see you disappear in a month."

"Okay," says Zoey. "Alright, I see your point. If you hire me and I decide to leave I'll give you proper notice, say two weeks. That's fair, isn't it?"

George sighs, knowing full well she could not refuse this opportunity if her life depended on it. Ever since this redhead strolled into her theatre, she's been hooked. Even two weeks is better than nothing. Why look a gift horse in the mouth? The girl is absolutely stunning. There is a future ahead of her much better than going back to some hick prairie town and giving it all up for an idiotic ex-boyfriend-boss named for a dead prophet. Obviously not an ideal situation or she wouldn't be out here on the run. If nothing else, taking this job might provide her escape from whatever mess she's gotten into back in Manitoba. George is no do-gooder but she does help out when she can. "It's a deal," she says briskly, resisting the urge to grasp Zoey's hand again. "You're hired."

They walk back without much conversation. George takes her backstage with simple instructions to help her get started, then returns quickly to her office to answer the telephone. "Vancouver Community Theatre," she says crisply.

"I want to speak to Zoey."

"Who is this?"

"Aren't you George?"

"Yes."

"You hired her, didn't you?"

"Yes. Yes I did."

"I thought you would. This is Elijah. Tell her I have to talk to her."

"Just a minute." George puts the call on hold and lays the receiver on her desk. Zoey is busily unrolling old posters. "There's a call for you in my office."

Zoey looks surprised. "Who'd call me here?"

"Who do you think? If you don't want to talk to him, I can say you've just stepped out."

"Oh shit, never mind. He'll just keep on pestering till I do. He can be real persistent, you have no idea." Stretching, she stands and follows George along the hallway.

"Line two," says George. "You'll want privacy. I'll go out and get us coffee."

"Make mine iced." She picks up the receiver. "Eli," she says. "How'd you get this number?"

When George returns she finds the girl slouched behind the desk. "Come on," she says cheerily. "Let's go outside. It's beautiful, the sun is shining. I'll show you my favourite patch of grass."

three wishes

Dear Eli,

I think I'm going to like this job. I can wear whatever I want — no office clothes!! — and I think George might become my friend. I sure wish you hadn't told her about us though, you could've screwed everything up for me. It's nobody's business, is it? That's what you always say anyway. I'm missing you like crazy. Every time I look at the mountains I wish you could see them too. It's all so beautiful, like being in a postcard. Oh yeah, I keep forgetting that you & what's-her-face came here for your honeymoon so of course you know all about it. My hair feels great! I think it's because of the water. I'm going to let it grow again. I really wish you'd write to me, even if it's just a memo. And in case you're wondering, which you're probably not, I still love you with all my heart and soul.

Zoey

whipping

George was born not able to distinguish people for whom she lusts by gender. It just happened that the first person she ever wanted was a girl, Gracie, in grade one nearly thirty years ago. But she's had boys too. It's a simple matter of who she wants at any given moment and at this moment who she wants is Zoey. Keeping polite employer hands to herself is wearing thin. They've worked side by side all week, an entire week without connecting once and now it's Friday afternoon and George is glumly contemplating another working weekend. She asks the girl to join her for a break outside.

"Sure thing." Zoey stands and dips into her denim pocket for a cigarette which she lights while stepping through the door George is holding open.

"Has anyone ever told you you smoke too much?" George asks, feeling too much like a mother and wishing she could bite back her words.

The girl blows a stream of rings, stabbing through them one by one with her forefinger. "Yeah," she says glumly. "I've been told, but thanks for asking. I have a question for you too. Have you ever had a boyfriend?"

George raises her brows. "I have one now. Why do you ask?"

"No reason," says Zoey vaguely. "Vibes, I guess. I've just been wondering."

"I've had boy and girlfriends both."

"Does that mean you're bisexual?"

George shrugs. "I suppose so, although I prefer to think of myself as person-specific."

"Oh. Have you got plans for the weekend?"

"Just work," answers George, heart beating wildly. "Writing. Work. Nothing I can't postpone."

"Are you working on another novel?"

"I'm always working on another novel."

"Can I read it?"

"No."

"Why not?"

"It isn't done. I never let anyone see my work in progress. I think I'm afraid I might change it to suit them and then I won't know if it's truly mine."

"Are you planning to be busy the whole weekend?"

"Why?"

"I thought maybe you and me could get together. Do something. I don't have anyone else to hang with here."

"Well," says George swiftly. "As I said, it's nothing that I can't postpone. I've been meaning to ask you over to my apartment for a home-cooked meal. You must be sick to death of restaurants."

"Eating out is not so bad and in this city there's a lot of choice. But I'd love to see your place."

"How about tomorrow? Around five-thirty?"

"Great! Is there anything I should bring?"

"Wine," says George. "If you want. I'm not particular. Buy whatever you prefer."

At home that evening she nervously rearranges furniture. It's how she does her housework, by moving things around. Friends can always tell if she has been cleaning by where the sofa is. As she works she plans the menu; she'll go to Granville Island in the morning for fresh salmon, nugget spuds and white asparagus. Planning chocolate mousse with whipped cream gets her going on what else she might do with chocolate, whipping cream and foxy Zoey.

dinner wine & roses

She arrives at five-thirty bearing dinner wine and roses. "Oh good, I've got the right apartment," she says when George opens the door. She thrusts a bottle at her. "Here's the wine. It might not be right for what you're making but it's my favourite. And some roses too. I couldn't resist the colour and they were so cheap. Wow! This is so cool! Can I look around?"

George accepts the gifts. "Sure, go ahead. I'll put these in water." She fills a vase while Zoey wanders through the front room looking at trinkets, photographs and full bookshelves, but doesn't touch a thing.

"This painting looks familiar. Is it you? Who did it?"

"Mmhmm, it's me and the artist's name is Nancy Rider. She's a former lover."

"Did she make this carving too?"

"No. That's from Riki."

"Another lover?" When George nods, Zoey snorts. "I guess that's one way to get an art collection. I can't make a goddamn thing. In case you're wondering."

George hides her grin among the coral blossoms. "I suppose I'll let you stay for dinner anyway."

"Is it alright for me to look in your other rooms?"

"If you promise not to damage my priceless lover-art," teases George.

"Hey!" protests Zoey. "I'm just looking." And disappears down the hallway.

George finds her in the bedroom gazing at a painting. Gently she sets a hand upon her shoulder. "That's the best one of the lot," she says softly. "Nancy's. It's called *blue nude*."

The girl turns, her green eyes full. "How does she do that?" she asks. "How can such a simple painting make me want to cry?"

George swallows hard. Zoey is so close. She smells so sweet. She is so impossibly naïve. Impulsively she reaches out. It's nothing, just a few swift strokes but she stops herself, steps quickly back trembling, and clears her throat. "Come keep me company," she says. "We'll open up that wine you brought and I'll finish making dinner."

In the kitchen she occupies her hands with preparations while Zoey perches on a stool drinking wine and chattering. But she eats silently and when her plate is clear she neatly lays her fork and knife across it. "That was really excellent! Where did you learn to cook like that?"

"I taught myself. I like doing it. It's fun and it relaxes me."

"Eli says that too. He's so good he could be a chef, but he's not allowed to do it at his house."

"Why ever not?"

"Because of Lori, that's his wife. She thinks it's faggy. He lets her make all the decisions about that kind of shit so he only cooks at my house now. I mean since they've been married. I can help you clean up. It's the only kitchen thing I'm good at doing."

"Alright," says George and together the two women clear the table, rinse and stack used dishes in the dishwasher.

"It's weird to be in an actual home. At the bed-and-breakfast I don't even have a kitchen. It makes me feel like a tourist."

"If you decide to stay you might want to look for an apartment. I could help," George offers. "There may be a vacancy in this building; I can check."

Zoey stretches. "I don't know why, but eating tires me right out. Eli thinks it's from allergies. Do you have an ashtray or should I smoke outside?"

"There's one in the living room. I thought we could watch a video."

"Cool. Which one?"

"Why don't you choose?"

Zoey paws through the collection and selects an Egoyan but within minutes she is sound asleep. George pulls an afghan up around her, turns off the television and crawls into her bed. Alone, with all her bloody memories.

restless cramps on Sunday

They first met when George hired her to design a set. She was an amazon and an artist and of course George fell instantly into heat. Her hands were constantly on Nancy. As it turned out, she was not the only one. As it turned out, the more people lusting after Nancy the happier she was. The more people groping at her body the better off her art. Every time George turned a corner she'd find her up against some wall or floor or piece of set humping someone's mouth or hair or crotch or fingers. "Georgie too," she'd say, making room somewhere on her body. Sharing her like that made George feel sick but more often than not she gave in, joining whoever was into Nancy at that moment, hoping she'd end up wanting her more than she wanted anybody else. "*Only* Georgie," she'd gasp in George's mind. It was so much easier to satisfy her in fantasy. But in reality it only happened once or twice, only after George discovered what made her goddess come so good she didn't ask for anybody else.

Sunday morning and she has been dreaming *Nancy*. She is licked with sweat, her stomach is in knots and she makes it to the toilet in the nick of time.

Zoey awakens to her retching. "Are you sick?" she asks from the doorway. "Do you want to be alone or can I help?"

George groans. "I just had a nightmare. Could you pass a washcloth?"

Zoey wets a cloth, wrings and passes it. "Does this happen often?"

"I don't get sick every morning if that is what you're asking." After Zoey leaves the room, George stands glaring at her own reflection. Brushes her teeth and rinses her mouth. Applies eyeliner, smudged so it's not too obvious. Of course Zoey looks fantastic. At nineteen everyone looks good, even after spending an entire night on someone else's sofa.

She prepares coffee while Zoey showers, checking off tourist sites for a rainy Sunday in her mind. Water pipes gargle as she chops mushrooms, shallots, black olives and red pepper. She crumbles in a bit of feta, reminding herself again of Nancy who once hurled an omelette at the wall enraged because she said feta made it taste like mouldy mouseshit. Nancy claimed her rage came from her father, the unknown artist whose most famous hanging was himself, from the sturdy rafters of his Manitoba studio. That dead daddy who she claims to love with all her heart and cunt and soul.

George serves Zoey who does not complain, who is towel-wrapped and shining, who eats with utter concentration. When the towel slips to expose her perfect breasts she does not pull it up. George sets down her mug with itchy fingers and clears her throat. "Do you want to go out with me today? See some sights?"

Zoey shrugs. "Where's that ashtray?"

"Probably where you left it, beside the couch." When she stands the towel slides to her hips and George must pretend those rosy nipples do not exist, nor that tiny waist nor the flawless ivory-toned skin nor the copper-brushed pubic thatch she senses faintly traced beneath white cotton. It's getting harder by the second, this being here with nearly-naked Zoey.

"I thought you had to work."

"Work can wait."

"It's raining."

"You're in Vancouver now," says George. "Get used to it."

"I don't know . . ." The girl pops her index finger through the smoke rings she is blowing. "I kinda got my period. I don't think I'm in much of a mood for seeing sights."

"There's tampons in the bathroom. Help yourself." George has awakened with voluptuous Nancy on her mind and now without Zoey to use as an eraser she'll be stuck with her all day. Driving around in dreary rain on a gloomy Sunday seems less appealing every minute. What she really needs is to get good and drunk.

As the fates would have it, Zoey emerges from the bathroom fully clothed and clutching her belly, white and moaning. "I can't hang out with you today," she groans. "I have to go."

George leaps to her feet and grabs her keys. "I'll drive you home."

Back at her bed-and-breakfast, Zoey drags upstairs to her room where she flops onto the bed. Stiff from George's couch and bloated from her period. She never got cramps before but now she has them all the time.

So now George finally knows where her pet employee lives and it's still Sunday and it's still raining. There's still the urgency of Nancy on her mind. She could call her up and they could fuck like in the bad old days. Nancy claims there are no good-byes, she is famous for it. But first George would have to shove her head inside a bottle. Which leaves her driving aimlessly past Wreck Beach, no doubt deserted under drizzle, restless with her memory.

At home she fills a glass with vodka and gets out her cardex pretending that she does not recall every stinking digit of the number off by heart. She takes a sip for each, and while Nancy's answering machine growls a generic sexy greeting, she gulps it down. "Hey there!" she says brightly. "It's me! Long time no see! Are you out of town or what? Call me. Anytime. If you still have my number. Ciao." Then she hangs up quickly. Her throat is parched, her heart is pounding and already she regrets her words. Miserably she peers out at the bleak grey sky draining endless rain into the endless water. The towel Zoey used unsuccessfully as a covering is lying on the floor where she dropped it. George drapes it around her shoulders and pours herself another drink. Smelling Zoey, thinking *Nancy*.

no good-byes

A weekend's worth of messages awaits her at the office Monday morning. Terry wants to come in for a sound check Thursday; Mario wants an estimate for a one-man show, how's December? Zoey mumbles she's too cramped up to work. Leslie has just graduated and wants to know if they're hiring.

"So sorry I missed your call," purrs Nancy. "Of course I have your number, silly."

"Zoey I have to talk to you! Phone me at the office; it's important!" Elijah says impatiently.

Not that Nancy's call means a goddamn thing. Since there are no good-byes where she's concerned, the two of them could pick up exactly where they left off as though nothing had ever changed between them. Because according to Nancy, nothing has.

At home she finds a parcel leaned against the door. She picks it up, lets herself in, peels off her damp socks and pours a drink. The box from the east-side sex shop Nancy favours contains a seductive, slender whip and a note penned in silver ink on black paper. All of this bears the too-familiar scent of Nancy courting. Now she sees her message light is flashing and she is scared to listen, terrified that she will hear the screaming, hear the sounds that Nancy used to make while fucking which have been heating her all day. She ignores her messages and decides instead to go check up on Zoey. Locks the door leaving her mementos safely on the other side.

The landlady says no guests allowed, but when George tells her Zoey is all alone and quite ill, she leads the way upstairs to where the girl lies glassy-eyed and prone upon her bed with the sheets pulled to her chin. "Have you taken anything?" George demands. "Tylenol? Aspirin?"

Zoey shakes her head violently with teeth clenched and chattering. So George winds her in a blanket and lugs her down the stairs and outside to her car. She calls Smitty on her cellphone, one advantage of having had a doctor as a lover, and when they arrive she is waiting at the clinic entrance.

"Who is she?" Smitty asks.

"Her name is Zoey; she's just moved out here from Manitoba. Her period started yesterday and she's been sick ever since. That's all I know."

"Probably needs a D&C." The doctor snaps on a pair of gloves. "I can do it here with a light sedative. Let's have a look hon. Lie back and don't you worry about a single thing. You'll be just fine." After she has finished cleaning Zoey's insides, Smitty helps carry her dopey patient to the car, whispering for George to call sometime.

At her apartment she hoists the girl into bed, folds the blanket over her, turns off the light and closes the door. Nancy's gift is on the table where she left it. When she lies upon the couch, when she shuts her eyes what she sees is Nancy.

There are times when life unfolds before your eyes, when everything in it stretches out ahead predictably like a prairie highway. Then there are other times when you are too blind to see your hand in front of your own face. She stumbles for the door in the middle of the night and there she is, crimson-lipped and raven-haired, the amazon of her dampest dreams barely clad in lace and leather. A blind moment. George braces herself against the wall.

"Aren't you going to ask me in?" Nancy pouts. "Or shall we do it in the hall?"

Trembling and without thought, George tugs her inside, kicking shut the door. Pushes Nancy hard the way she likes it, rubs her eager thighs, spreads the lips she can pretend are hungry just for her. Pulls her to the table where she fumbles for the whip. But all at once her prairie highway stretches clear ahead.

"Hurry," Nancy says impatiently. "Do it! Now!"

"No," says George. "You could at least act as though you care it's me. Kiss me, something! Christ! I haven't even touched you in over half a year."

Nancy sticks out her tongue. "You must have heard my messages. You got the gift I had delivered, didn't you?"

"I got them," George says heavily. "But I'm not sure I understand what they mean."

"What they mean," Nancy says, "is that I missed you."

"You did," says George roughly. Then, with two firm hands, she urges Nancy to her knees. "Show me," she growls. The thought of Nancy pleasing her for once is so exciting that she comes almost right away. That's when she remembers Zoey in the other room. Flushed and panting she forces the woman to her feet. "You have to leave!" she says. "You have to go right now!"

"What the fuck is up with you?" Nancy demands. "We haven't even started yet."

"There's someone in my bedroom."

"Ahhh!"

"It's not like that."

"What is it like then?"

George shrugs. "Just this sick kid I'm taking care of."

"Let's have a look," says Nancy.

She starts across the room with George following close behind. "Don't!" she protests but the woman is already at the bedroom door. With her boot she nudges it and there is Zoey sound asleep upon her belly, her bare back sloping into gentle hill of unspoiled buttock covered with the sheerest panty silk.

Nancy draws a ragged breath. "Mmmm," she hums as the girl rolls onto her back.

George sees what Nancy sees, tiny breasts, taut nipples, stomach hard and flat, and she clenches a tight hand around her elbow. "Come on! Let's go! She isn't well."

Nancy pivots. "You never were any good at sharing," she hisses.

"No," says George. "No. I'm not."

"Too bad. Because I wouldn't mind a piece of that. I wouldn't mind at all." Then to George's great relief she strides towards the door, picking up the whip as she passes it. "I'll call again," she says firmly.

Wordlessly George watches Nancy strutting down the vacant hallway snapping aimless leather at other people's doors.

games

Restlessly George prowls her apartment. The thought of Nancy having been here is so unbelievable that by dawn she wonders if she imagined the entire thing. Out of lust or boredom or loneliness, it can happen. But the empty gift box and the note assure her that she wasn't dreaming. She pulls a chair beside the bed to watch as Zoey struggles up from sleep. "Good morning," she says softly when the girl's eyes open.

"Oh hi," says Zoey. "I couldn't remember where I was. What did that doctor do to me?"

"You had some blockage in your uterus so she did a D&C."

"I was really scared."

"So was I, but you're going to be just fine. I'll run you a bath and I've made broth. Which do you want first?"

"Broth, I think. My mouth tastes like a sewer."

George brings soup, fluffs pillows and fills the tub. All day she hovers over Zoey who, by mid-afternoon, is lounging on the couch in flannel PJs playing video games.

"Don't you have to work today?" she asks, annoyed.

"I thought I'd stay here to take care of you. Why?"

"Your fussing makes me nervous. You're acting like a mother. Shit! I died." She starts another game.

George picks up the phone on the second ring.

"About last night . . ." Nancy croons. "It was fantastic! I mean seeing you again. I hadn't realised how very much I've missed you."

"As evidenced by your constant effort to stay in touch with me," says George wryly. "Your persistence has been overwhelming."

"Whatever." Nancy giggles. "I was thinking we didn't get to do much catching-up last night. What with one thing leading to another . . ."

"We didn't get to much of anything."

"So tell me, are you still at the theatre? Because I'm between commissions at the moment and I was thinking why not do some set design? It would keep me active and exercise those muscles. Right now I can work practically pro bono. Better grab it while you can. It's a one-time-only offer!"

Zoey tosses the game control to the floor and stands up stretching.

"Don't you have a show coming up?"

"You mean the one in May? I was sure I had you on the guest list. You really should've come. The critics raved about the nudes and they sold like mad. So what about some work?"

"We can't afford you. Everyone in theatre is in cutback mode."

"Really? I didn't know. I've had a terrific year."

"I'm going back to bed," Zoey whispers.

George covers the receiver. "I'll be in soon with your medicine."

"What's that?" Nancy asks.

"I'm playing nurse."

"Can I play too?"

"No."

"Seriously, when will I see you?"

"Seriously, never."

"Nothing heavy. No commitment."

"That's what I'm not ready for."

"Don't be too quick to answer. Mull it over. And remember, I'll work practically for free."

holding

When Zoey awakens from her nap it's early evening. She pokes her head around the doorway of the den where George is busy at her computer. "Can I use your phone?" she asks.

"Of course," says George. "You needn't ask permission."

"I'm calling Eli. It's long-distance."

"Which reminds me, he left a message for you at the theatre. He said that it was urgent."

"Urgent!" Zoey sniffs. "He's just pissed because he doesn't have me at his beck and call. Can I use the phone in your room? I'll call collect."

George nods. "That's fine," she says absently.

Eli answers on the first ring. "Why am I paying for this?" he demands after he accepts the charges. "You're the one with the inheritance. Where the hell have you been? How come no one ever answers at the theatre? I've been leaving messages."

"I'm warning you," says Zoey. "If you just want to bitch at me I'm hanging up."

"I hate not being able to talk to you when I want. Where are you anyway?"

"At my boss's place."

"What are you doing over there?"

"I'm sick and she didn't want me to be alone so I'm staying here till I get better."

"Sick how?"

"Some kind of infection in my uterus. The doctor gave me a prescription."

"When are you coming home?"

"I've got a job now, El."

"This new girl of ours isn't working out at all; she's driving us insane. Jer and me both want you back."

"That's all you need me for?" asks Zoey softly. "To do your filing?"

"You know what I mean."

"Why can't you just say it?"

"I don't know. Because I can't."

She picks up a fluffy pillow and heaves it at the bedroom door. "You can't say you love me and besides, you have a wife."

"At least I don't bullshit you. I never bullshit you."

"So what? You expect brownie points for that?"

"So I've never pretended; I've never lied. I never promised you a fucking thing."

"Is that supposed to be some kind of comfort?"

"You don't understand."

"You're not so special El; an awful lot of married guys fuck around."

"I phoned to tell you that I'm coming out to get you. I'll be there on Friday. I've already bought my ticket and it's non-refundable so you may as well give me your address."

"You can't just come out here!"

"If you won't tell me, I'll find out anyway. I know where you work; I'll just look it up in the book." He sounds so smug. "You're not as lost as you'd like to think. It's the Vancouver Community Theatre, am I right?"

"I could disappear by Friday."

"But you won't."

Zoey winds the cord coils around her fingers one at a time. "What about your wife?"

"She thinks I'm going to a conference on the coast."

"She doesn't know I'm out here, does she?"

"It wouldn't matter if she did."

That means he's made excuses to his wife, and even though Zoey knows he's lying about it not mattering if she finds out, she also knows she's been defeated. She gives him the address of the theatre, hangs up and lies back listlessly, barely acknowledging George's knock.

She enters, stooping to pick up the tossed pillow, then perches with it on the bed. "You really ought to get some rest. You look exhausted."

"Eli's coming," Zoey says.

"He's coming here? When?"

"This Friday. He's going to try to force me to go back with him."

"Didn't you tell him that you're sick?"

"I told him but he doesn't give a shit. He only cares about himself."

George leans forward, stroking Zoey's hair. "Poor baby," she says soothingly and waits a few moments for the rhythmic breath of sleep. Zoey is in her bed, but Nancy's on her mind. She should go out and find someone she knows to get laid with but she cannot leave the girl alone. Nancy might show up again. And besides it's Tuesday and no one goes out on Tuesday, they rent videos. She shuts down her computer, switches off the lights and lies upon the couch but soon she is aroused by sobbing. She hurries back to kneel beside the bed. "Sweetie, what's the matter? Can I get you something?"

"I just want someone to hold me," Zoey moans.

So George holds on and eventually they sleep, sandwiched in each other's arms.

The first thing she notices is sunlight squeezing through the blinds; the second is the body spooning hers. A hot mouth upon her shoulder, timid fingers toying with her vulva. George is suddenly afraid to breathe, terrified the girl will awaken fully to perhaps regret the moves her body has been making. Then one wiggling finger finds her clit.

"If I kept doing this, would you come?" asks Zoey hoarsely.

"That should do it," mutters George. Waves of lust wash through her. Shafts of sunlight splash on Nancy's nude. Zoey's breasts pressing hard against her back. She should say something, wake her up, make sure she knows what she's getting herself into. But then Zoey pushes the heel of her hand down hard and George thinks *this could go on forever, I wouldn't mind, I wouldn't mind at all*. Zoey laps the corner of her mouth. Soft lips, eager flesh, no more thinking is required.

Sated, Zoey rests her head on George's outstretched arm. "That was nice," she says shyly. "I've wanted to do it for the longest time, ever since we met. I just didn't think I'd have the nerve."

"Same here."

"Really? Did I do it right?"

"You did it perfectly."

"I didn't know I could."

"Didn't know that you could what?"

"Have an orgasm. I had one, right?"

"Why do you ask? Haven't you had one before?"

Zoey turns away. "Uh-uh."

"Never?"

"Not that I know of."

"Not in your entire life?"

"Could you just hold onto me?" Zoey asks, embarrassed. "Please?"

the only one

By the time George awakens, Zoey has left the bed. She finds her seated on the couch, smoking. When she leans down for a kiss the girl turns away, and after a silent hurried breakfast she urges George through the doorway saying she'll be fine alone, not to worry. During her walk to work George mulls it over. Maybe she didn't realise what she was doing earlier. Maybe she needs time to think over what, if anything, it means, her first time with a woman. Perhaps she is frightened or ashamed, and in denial. At the office, she checks her e-mail and messages. Nancy has left another offer of cheap labour. She must be in a dry spell, between shows, between lovers. Most likely she is simply bored. George imagines Zoey's body under Nancy's expert hands and the stunning image she would create from it. Briefly the idea excites her, but thinking about what else she might do with it is too disturbing for even passing fantasy. George sets her boots upon the desk and leans back in her chair. Lost in thought, she jumps when heavy hands settle on her shoulders.

"Guess who?" booms a familiar voice.

She drops the pen she has seized and is holding like a weapon. "Jean Paul!" she shouts. "You're back!"

"How did you know it was me?" he asks.

"Who else could it be? How was Paris?"

"You should've been there; it was divine. The French worship me and you know what adoration does to my sex drive! You missed a golden opportunity to get fucked. Royally."

"So tell me who you fucked instead."

"A bevy of beauties were spread out across the city just for me."

"I hope you used condoms."

"Actually I exaggerate. Truth be told I only fucked Marie and then I had to pay extra for the rubber."

"You paid for it?"

"As I said, you should have been there. And how has your love-life been? Dismal, don't I wish."

George sighs. "I've gone and done something really stupid. I've hired myself practically-a-virgin help."

"And you just can't wait to rub it in, can you?"

"Wait a minute! You asked! Anyway, what about Marie?"

"Tut-tut. Not a fair comparison, not at all. Come away with me fair maiden so I can ply you with caffeine and you will tell me about your nymphet."

"I really shouldn't. I've been slacking off all week."

"Not with me, you haven't. I've missed you, my girl. When oh when will you make an honest man of me?"

George stands quickly, dislodging grasping hands. "Oh don't!" she says impatiently.

Jean Paul frowns. "Don't what?"

"Go spoiling our time together with pressure about that."

"Neither of us is getting younger; we haven't got forever to decide."

"Since when have you been speaking in clichés?"

"Since always. I thought you liked it."

"Well I don't." She hoists her bag across one shoulder. "I thought you were taking me away from all of this."

At the café they take their cappuccino to an outside table where he lights a cigarette and then leans forward. "Now. Tell Papa all about the help and don't spare me any juicy detail."

"Not this minute," hedges George.

"Have a heart! I've been away for two entire months! Surely you can't begrudge me a bit of gossip."

George shuffles salt and pepper packets. "If it's gossip that you want, I've heard from Nancy."

"Don't tell me you're into that again!"

"I'm not into anything! Let's just say she's been around. She says she wants to do some set design and claims she'll work for next to nothing."

"Good old Nancy Rider!" he says scornfully. "Pornographer to the rich and famous."

George shrugs. "I have no idea what she's selling. She said her show in May was sensational for sales."

With effort, he relaxes. "Never mind; not important. So . . . The nymphet?"

"Zoey," George says softly. "Very sweet. Nineteen. A green-eyed red-headed prairie gal. Gorgeous, although she totally doesn't know it yet. She came looking for a job and I hired her."

He snorts. "Naturally!"

"Just a second, there's a story here. Her ex-boss is also her ex-lover and he wants her back. The hitch is that he's married. But he's still coming out this weekend to try to talk her into going home with him."

"Does he know baby bear's been lapping at your porridge?"

"The guy's straight-edged, he doesn't know from porridge."

"Ah-hah." Jean Paul grins but his eyes are cold. "So she has!"

George balls a fist and pummels his sleeve with it. "You always do this to me! First you coax me into telling and then you get jealous. What are you anyway, some kind of masochist?"

"I must be," he says morosely. "Since I'm with the only woman I'll ever love, grilling her for sordid details about her other lovers . . . Why do I do this to myself? Because I keep hoping against all reason that someday you'll come to your senses long enough to realise I'm the only one for you. Never mind masochism, what sort of idiot am I?"

George lifts her palms. "I don't make any secret of my needs."

"Of what you think you need," he says. "But do you actually know what you want? If you could tell me absolutely that there isn't any hope for us, I could try to find another soulmate. I doubt it's possible, but I could try."

"Let's see those reviews," suggests George.

"Not too subtle babe."

"We've been together for barely twenty minutes and we're already arguing. Just be nice for once!"

When George gets angry, Jean Paul gets tired. Now he yawns. "What I think is you're past thirty while she is still a child with a boyfriend who intends to drag her back to Mudsville. You're out of your league, that's all I'm saying."

"For your information I did not seduce her, although I must admit to being willing. Besides it only happened once."

"So she wanted to experiment and you just happened to be available. You're so easy it's disgusting."

George shifts. "I should get back to work. Show me your reviews."

He smirks. "I see I hit a nerve. Okay, so twist my arm."

"Don't tempt me."

He sets his attaché case on the table and with a flourish opens it. "Which first?"

"Which do you like best?"

"Here, read this. It's the only one in English."

"'Exquisite . . . effervescent . . . flamboyant!' This is fabulous!"

"I'm taking the rest in for translation. But they're all enthusiastic."

George checks her watch and rises. "I really should get back now."

"We're going out tonight," says Jean Paul.

"I'm not sure . . ."

"Your place, nine-ish, dress for dinner," he says firmly. "And I won't take no for an answer."

George leaves him on the corner crouched to shield his lighter from the breeze.

When she returns from work she finds Zoey passed out on the couch snoring through her mouth and clutching at the game control. She tiptoes past her to check messages, then she fills the tub and pours herself a glass of wine. Cliché thoughts like *it never rains but pours, either feast or famine* spring to mind. She's had a long famished summer and all at once there is all this. A sexy child in her bed, her goddess Nancy on her stoop and Jean Paul being as attentive as he's ever been. She drains the tub, pats on moisturiser, brushes through her hair and applies brash makeup. That done, she gently rubs Zoey's cheek.

"What's the time?" The girl awakens grumbling.

"It's eight-thirty. How are you?"

Zoey stretches, baring two pert nipples. "I missed you," she complains. "Where have you been all day?"

"Make up your mind! Yesterday you wanted to get rid of me because of my mothering and this morning you all but pushed me out. Where are your clothes?"

"It's much too hot for clothes. Besides, I've had a fever."

George's greedy fingers graze the supple skin. "I'm expecting my date in, let's see," she says, tweaking a chubby breast. "Mmmm. Fifteen minutes."

Zoey giggles. "Then don't start something you can't finish."

"I won't." She wrests her hand away and stands. "Are you sure that you're alright?" she asks softly. "I mean about this morning."

"I don't see a problem." The girl shrugs. "Do you?"

When Jean Paul pulls up in his Jag, George is waiting in the lobby. Darting out through pelting rain, she slides in and pecks his cheek. They eat dinner while he chatters on about the relative merits of European art, his show, Paris and his future plans while George nods and chews and smiles.

"You're coming home with me," he says over their dessert. "You can't refuse, I've been away for much too long. Plus I have been mostly celibate."

"Nearly," she says. "Me too."

"And you owe me for this dinner."

"Which is it you expect, a mercy fuck or a reward?"

The house is musty from being closed all summer. "You sit tight while I take care of this," he says, rushing to open windows. "You could pour us drinks."

George finds wine chilling and fills two glasses. Then she slides off her panties, crumples them into a ball which she tucks beneath a cushion, and sits. He returns, standing back from her, holding heavy fingers against pursed lips. All she can think about right now is those delicious digits poking into her; there's something absolutely sexy about a man who has to have you. Squirming, she spreads her legs and he kneels between them, setting his hands firmly on her knees. She manages to sip her wine as though nothing else exists, but when his tongue finds her clit she has to gasp.

He lifts his head. "What was that?" he asks.

"Not a thing," she says primly. One button at a time she opens up her blouse. "I may have spilled a bit of wine."

"Messy girl!" he chides. "Now I'll have to clean you up. Where exactly did you spill?"

"Here," she pouts, pointing to her breast. Meticulously he licks a circle around her nipple. "And see what else you've done," she scolds. "You've made me wet all over."

"Specifically where are you wet?" he asks hoarsely.

Again she points. "Here. And here as well."

With his free hand he tugs down his zipper and steps from his jeans. Then piece by careful piece he removes her clothing. Pre-come tears are leaking from his cock but still he pushes her away, positions her, steps back with folded arms across his chest and George knows exactly what he wants. Setting fingers on herself, she teases open her fat pussy. While she massages, he nods and smiles and when next she reaches he fills her quickly. After he is spent, he lays his head on her, idly scraping fingertips along her vulva. "You absolutely have to marry me," he whispers. "We're so perfect for each other. You cannot keep me hanging. You cannot keep on saying no."

His nails are chafing. She shudders, pushing off his hand. "I much prefer it this way," she says. "There's no reason for us to ruin what we have with marriage."

"You haven't given us a chance. There's always someone else on your horizon."

"You're much too possessive as it is."

"I am not possessive! Merely insanely jealous."

"Then you'd be insane with jealousy all the time. Plus you'd think you had a right. I don't believe in marriage, you know that."

"Maybe you wouldn't want the others. Maybe I would be enough."

"Why are you laying this on me again? Why do you insist on spoiling such a lovely evening?"

"I'm sorry, I can't seem to help myself. Are you staying? Because if you are, I'm going to brush my teeth and if not, I'll help you find your clothing and drive you home like the gentleman I am."

collection

George sleeps fitfully beside Jean Paul and by sunrise she is wide awake and wild with guilt over having left the child alone. Hurriedly she gathers up her clothing, stumbles into it and leaves.

At her apartment, she finds cool-skinned Zoey in her bed. "Who's there?" she croaks.

"Shhh," says George. "It's only me. Everything's alright. Go back to sleep."

"Is it morning? Where have you been all night?"

"I'm sorry; I forgot about the time."

"I was worried."

"But you're okay."

"Now that you're here, I am. Georgie?"

"What?"

"Come here."

"I don't have the time. I have to get ready to go to work."

Zoey squints up at the window. "But it's barely dawn." She reaches out to tug on George's skirt like a toddler wanting something. "I missed you," she insists.

"I have to take a shower," George protests. "I've got a busy day ahead."

Zoey's palm cups her vulva. "My pussy is all wet," she says. "From thinking about you. I don't want you to leave."

"I really should," says George reluctantly, tugging down her skirt and stepping through it.

"I never knew," sighs Zoey, watching. "I never thought a woman could be so pretty down there. I guess that's what Eli sees when he looks at me."

And after all, George is only human. When someone young and beautiful is worshipping her body she doesn't necessarily have the heart to make them stop. She bends down for a simple kiss which becomes a tonguing, then a fondle, followed by rough thrashing. This girl knows precisely where to put her fingers for George to come all over them.

So she is late for her meeting after all and the clown with whom she's dealing is irate. But she wins him over with her charm and later in the day a messenger arrives with a large package, the gift of a flamboyant oil courtesy of Jean Paul, which she hangs on the wall across from her desk where she will see it all the time. After work she finds him leaned against his car waiting just for her.

At the sight of her, he bounces like a boy. "Did you get my present? Did ya, huh?"

"It's wonderful! Thanks a million."

"Consider it an investment."

"Naturally. That's how I consider all my art. Where exactly are we going?"

"I'm taking you out dancing. But first we have to get you properly attired." He opens the passenger door of his Jag and ushers her inside. At her building he shifts into park. "You'd probably prefer to have me wait."

"You could come up," she says. "Have some wine. I'll be awhile."

Zoey, mercifully dressed for a change and curled up on the couch watching television, leaps to attention when they enter. She shoves out her hand. "I'm Zoey," she says. "I guess she's told you all about me."

"I doubt if all," he says dryly. "For example, I didn't realise you were living here."

"That's because I'm not. I got sick and she offered to take care of me. Are you another artist friend?"

"How did you guess?"

"She's got this art collection."

He snorts. "I'm well aware of that."

"Do you know Nancy too?"

"I'm going to get changed," coos George. "Zoey, meet Jean Paul. I'll leave the two of you to get acquainted."

When she returns they're sharing reefer and Jean Paul pats the couch cushion between them, coughing. He holds the spliff to her lips, then passes it to Zoey who inhales dreamily, then drops her hand on George's thigh. "I called Eli this morning," she says. "I told him that I think I might be queer."

George sputters smoke. "Why in heaven's name would you tell him that?"

"Because. I think maybe I am."

"What else did you say to him?"

"Why are you so freaked? It's not like this has anything to do with you."

"You didn't mention me?"

Zoey snorts. "Of course not! I'm not completely stupid! I just told him how I've been thinking about things, like him always telling me I'm frigid."

"What did he say to that?" Jean Paul asks.

"He got so mad! First he told me that I'm not. Queer, I mean. He still thinks I'm frigid. Then he said homosexuality is a perversion and that my being here is giving me ideas and that this all goes to show why it's time for him to come and take me home."

"The boy's an idiot," says George fuzzily. There's fur gathering on her tongue from the pot and Zoey's childish patter and the constant kneading fingers on her leg are wreaking havoc with her mind.

"He said it's all the more reason for him to come out here."

"I don't get it," George says. "Why tell him?"

"I have to talk to someone," Zoey says defensively. "He's my only friend. I always tell him everything."

Jean Paul lays a sturdy arm across George's shoulders and fiddles idly with her nipple. He clears his throat. "I'll put on some music. Turn off that television, would you love?"

"*Love*," George repeats. "You sound so very European. No one would ever guess you were born right here. On the wet west coast of Canada."

"I was born in Manitoba," Zoey offers.

"I know, she told me." He smirks. "She tells me everything. Go on now dearie, turn it off."

Zoey aims the remote and the television image dies.

"Music," George reminds, licking her cracked lips. "And wine, be sweet JP. Get wine." He leaves the room while Zoey's hand inches farther up her thigh. "I have this surprise for you," she whispers. "But it's for later. I didn't expect you'd be bringing him."

"You should not be doing that," says George hoarsely.

Zoey's lashes flutter. "Doing what?"

"You know what. Because he gets insanely jealous."

"I'm not doing anything."

"That's hardly nothing. That's my cunt."

Zoey grabs her hand and, giggling, sets it palm-down on her lap. Something hard and cylindrical is pushing out beneath her stretchy miniskirt. "I'll bet mine is bigger than his is," she brags.

"What is that?" George asks.

"You should know. It's yours. I found it in your drawer."

Jean Paul returns with wine. "What did you just say?"

"I told her I bet mine is bigger than yours is," repeats Zoey boldly.

He stoops to give them each a glass and then passes a newly lit joint to George while Zoey stands, tugging up her spandex to show her strapon. "You see?" she asks, grinning.

"Mine is bigger," Jean Paul says thickly. "Without a doubt."

Zoey sets a hand upon her slender hip and fiddles with the dildo. "Prove it!" she demands.

Through a haze, George watches Jean Paul rise. Undo his fly. Step out of his jeans. Stroke his gradually stiffening penis. "It gets much bigger," he mutters, "when it's completely hard."

Zoey crinkles up her nose. "Let me see!" she exclaims. "Oh look! It's all wrinkly."

"At least it's real! At least it's not moulded plastic!"

George stubs the roach while her two lovers compare their dicks. She feels hot and restless so she unzips her dancing dress, tugging down thin straps to free her tingling breasts. Gradually she becomes aware of Zoey shoving at Jean Paul.

"Don't!" she shouts. "I don't want you to! I don't want to fuck with you!"

Quickly George jumps up, standing between the two of them, pushing him back with the flat of her hand. "Leave her alone!" she shouts. "Can't you hear? She told you, *no!*"

Jean Paul holds up two palms. "Truce!" he growls. "Peace! I get your point!" He slumps to the floor.

"It's just that I've been sick," Zoey whimpers. "Does he know that?"

George wraps her arms around the girl. "Don't worry," she says. "He won't do anything if you don't want him to. I promise." Then she slips to the floor, pulling Zoey with her. She lays her head on Jean Paul's lap, squirming lightly while he gently grasps and pins her arms. His prick is heavy underneath her. He shoves the bodice of her dress down to her waist and Zoey tugs it to her ankles, strips it from her feet and tosses it.

"Now may I fuck you?" she asks politely.

"I'd like that," George answers through the gauze her tongue is wrapped in.

"Then say *yes please.*"

"Yes. Please."

"Say *fuck me Zoey,*" commands Jean Paul.

"Fuck me Zoey," George repeats, feeling stretched. She waits for the girl to straddle her, and while Jean Paul scrubs her tits with two hard hands, Zoey pokes her cunt inexpertly. When she tumbles off he takes over, inserts his prick while Zoey rubs her clit between her fingertips. The two of them keep going at her until at last George crumples, whimpering. Satisfied.

honeymoon

George drags a strand of brass-licked hair around her index finger. "We really should get up," she says lazily. "Today's the day; Elijah's coming. Have you decided yet what you're going to do?"

"I'll probably stay at his hotel."

"Don't forget, I need you for the show this weekend."

"I know. I'll be there."

"I don't want him around."

"Don't you worry about a thing! I can twist him around my little finger."

The morning's work progresses smoothly and by mid-day Zoey has managed to move all the remaining clutter into the storage room. Nancy has called and George has told her nothing has come up but she'll let her know if something does. Jean Paul phones and whispers sweet endearments. George shows Zoey how to handle credit card transactions, where to put the cash and what to do with ticket stubs, then they take their lunch together. George is unusually pensive and eating in silence is always Zoey's habit.

After polishing her plate, she lights a smoke and suddenly she titters. "I was just thinking," she says, "about what El would say if I told him what you and me and old JP did last night."

George groans. "Aw, don't tell him! Please! He would never understand."

"Maybe it would turn him on, you never know."

"On the other hand, he might try to kill you. That's just it; you never know."

"You could be right." Zoey stubs her cigarette and stands. "I should get back to the theatre. He's probably already there."

He's not, but he soon arrives and since Zoey has retreated, George is left to greet him. Tall and lanky with a sexy hank of hair boldly thrust across one eye. In a well-cut business suit with a flashy Disney tie he's not at all the country bumpkin she has been expecting.

"Are you George?" he asks.

She recognises the husky voice. "And you are . . ." she says.

"Looking for Zoey."

"Why don't you take a seat?"

"No thanks." He grins. "My butt is sore. I've been sitting down all day. First the drive to Winnipeg and then the flight and then the taxi. Where is she?"

"Just hold on then while I tell her you've arrived. Elijah, right?"

Zoey is seated cross-legged on the floor, staring at the stacks of paper that surround her. Seeing George, she leaps to her feet and dashes down the hallway while her boss follows close behind. Elijah gathers Zoey in his arms, and after hugging him she leans back inside their possessive cradle. "How was your flight?" she asks him breathlessly. "Did you find a room? How long will you be staying?"

"Hang on a second, baby!" He disengages her and turns to George, glowering from the doorway. "Hey there boss-lady," he says sweetly. "Does she have to stay and be your drudge or can she come out and play with me?"

George crosses her arms. "I need to have her back by six."

"Thanks a million, George! I owe you one!" Zoey smacks into the air beside her cheek before the two of them race out like naughty children playing hooky.

At five o'clock she sits alone in the theatre, empty, waiting like a lover to be filled, picking soggy lettuce from her pita. The troupe straggles slowly in while anxiously she eyes the clock. But Zoey is on time as usual.

"Hi," she says, flinging mist from her umbrella. "I'm not late, am I? What should I be doing? I have tickets to get ready, right? Where is that cash box?" She chases frantically about before she settles in the booth beside the door.

After checking in to make sure she has everything she needs, George goes into her office, shuts the door, picks up her phone and dials. "Busy tonight?" she asks lightly.

Jean Paul chuckles. "I'm never busy, not where you're concerned. Why?"

"You could pick me up from work around eleven."

"Is something wrong?"

"I just want to spend the night with you. Do I need a reason?"

Late that evening in a hotel bed high above downtown streets Zoey contemplates a boring ceiling. The outer wall of the room is shrouded with ostentatious drapery hiding the spectacular mountain view. There is an upholstered armchair in a corner which could be dragged over to the window but she doesn't feel a bit like moving. This, as Eli recalled with prompting, is the exact same hotel where he and Lori spent their honeymoon. Zoey recognised the name. Even though she tells herself she expects nothing from him, what seems more true is that that is what he gives her. Nothing. Worse than nothing, bits and pieces. Keeps her dangling from a thread. Being on the edges of his life makes her feel like dryer lint, charcoal-grey and fuzzy. Maybe what he wants from her is filling for the spaces he leaves deliberately around himself. Maybe the reason he is here is because he misses her shadow in the corner of his eye where it's always been before.

How can he lie here sleeping? She sets a hand upon his body, at least its warmth assures her that he is alive. Beyond him on the bedside table are roses that he bought for her. Beyond them is the bathroom door ajar, the light on still from when she went to don her diaphragm. Children are for the wife and not the mistress, she knows this now. He told her he was tired, that he had a hellish week on top of getting ready for this trip, as though it were her fault. Her fingers tiptoe down his skin. It would be easy to go back home with him, much easier than staying here in this strange city trying to understand, trying to get a handle on the world. She has no life of her own here, not yet, no apartment and not a single stick of furniture. No one to notice if she went back with him right now except for maybe Georgie.

But he won't put her in the centre of his life. He uses her like a kitchen when he needs a place to cook, he uses her to answer the office phone, do the payroll, books and filing, he uses her for getting laid when and where he wants it. She wishes he would wake up now. "Eli!" she says urgently. He rolls over so her hand slides onto his chest and she shakes him. "Wake up. I have to talk to you!"

He groans. "Is it time for me to go already?"

"You're in Vancouver. You're not going anywhere."

"Then let me get some sleep."

"I don't want you to sleep. We have to talk."

"We've got all weekend."

"You'll keep putting it off and then you'll leave without us settling anything."

He sits, pulling the pillow up behind him with a grunt. "Jeez," he grumbles reaching for a cigarette. "There isn't anything to settle. You're coming home with me."

"We haven't discussed it."

"What's there to discuss?"

"I've got a new life here."

"This is not a life. You're just wasting time."

"How is me living my own life a waste of time?"

He sighs and smoothes the sheet crisply across his belly where he sets the ashtray. "I've told you and I've told you, I'm here to take you home."

"Telling is definitely not the same as asking."

"Okay, alright already, then I'm asking." He slings his arm around her. "Come home with me."

"You want us to go on the way we've always been? With me on the sidelines of your life as a convenience?"

"I see no reason for anything to change."

"You call my leaving you no reason?"

"You're the one who's been following me around since we were in high school."

"If I'm the follower, then why are you out here?"

"I knew this would happen if we started talking. You always rearrange the facts."

She leans forward. "Light me up a smoke."

Eli spreads his hand upon her shoulder and tugs lightly at her hair. "I really hate it when we fight," he says softly. "I've missed you way too much. Let's try not to spoil it."

With effort, Zoey swallows her hard anger down. "Okay," she says contritely. "Okay, I'll try."

yin to yang

Jean Paul picks her up from work, they go for drinks and then back to her place where in a minute he is snoring. She nudges him into bed, puts on her flannel PJs and settles in beside him with a paperback. Then, flushing out irritating imaginings of Zoey with another lover, she sleeps too and awakens to his hands becoming quickly indispensable. There's his solid body, his weight and heat, and his steady throbbing which makes her bottom out all at once.

"You know what I like about doing this with you?" she asks, catching her breath.

He rolls his arm underneath her neck and pulls her close. "What's that?"

"I like it that you don't fall asleep right after you've come. You hang in there with me. Not many males do that."

He sniffs. "You might say something ego-building about my apparatus, it wouldn't kill you. The rest is practise and seniority."

"Apparatus is aesthetic, it's nice but not absolutely necessary."

"Next you'll give me that old cliché that it's not what you have but how you use it."

"It works for me."

"What works for you doesn't count. You're not normal. You fuck with women."

"So do you."

"But I'm supposed to, it's natural. Yin to yang."

"Even animals have same-gender sex, if you want to bring up so-called laws of nature."

He reaches past her for his cigarettes. "Animals only do it when they're desperate."

"Not true, some use the other gender only for procreation. And certain species live in same-sex packs and do it with each other just for recreation."

"Never mind trying to convert me. If I were female I'd be as bi as you. And I don't care if you fuck other women, I just want us to get married."

He flicks his lighter and inhales. "What if we were to agree you could have as many lovers as you want with no recrimination?"

"What would be the purpose, given those conditions?"

"Mutual satisfaction." He rubs his prickly chin. "I want a wife and you need money. I've given this a lot of thought."

"Are you proposing open marriage?"

"You might call it that."

"Would we live together?"

"Yes, we'd live together and I would support your work so you wouldn't have to go on being an office hack fulfilling other people's dreams and filling in these crappy applications for paltry grants so you can write a little on the side."

His hair is more than streaked with silver. "Can you afford it?" asks George.

"Let's just say I'm comfortable; I own my house thanks to Father and the rest is pure gravy. Money is so easy to accumulate."

"So I could write full-time, have freedom without remorse and you'd support my work?"

"That's what I'm prepared to offer."

"And you say you've thought this through."

"As much as possible, I have."

"I'd be crazy to refuse." George leans back against the headboard. "Would there be a contract?"

"Naturally. I've drawn up a few rough drafts," he answers. "Well?"

She fiddles idly with his penis curled upon a nest of wiry pubic hair.

"I'll have to think it over."

Jean Paul grins. "Finally! Some progress! At least it's not an outright no this time." He stubs his cigarette, wrestles her down, grabs her hair and tugs on it while spending himself inside her mouth.

babe

Eli checks his shutter speed, then holds the camera to his face. "Stay right there," he orders. "I'm going to take your picture naked."

Zoey freezes in mid-step for just a second. Then she grabs the towel she draped across the chair after her shower and knots it quickly around her waist. "Don't!" she says. "I'm way too fat."

"No one will ever see it, I'll hide it at the office. Besides, you aren't fat. Come on!"

Stubbornly she sets her chin. "Absolutely not!" she snaps. But he lunges forward, tugs off the towel, aims and shoots. "It won't turn out," she says angrily. "You were much too close."

He tosses the camera on the bed. "No one gives a shit about your fat, it's not what we'll be looking at, you know." He winks, then snaps his fingers. "Come on, get dressed, let's go! I have an appointment to test-drive an XK8."

They take a taxi to the import dealer where she hangs around outside smoking while Eli goes in to kick some tires. At last he pulls up in an elegantly sleek red Jaguar. "Hop in," he says. "I got her for the weekend. She's so sexy! Sweet as sin."

"How much?" asks Zoey glumly.

"About a hundred twenty K Canadian," Eli says. "Well worth it, every penny. But no gear shift, it'll take some getting used to."

Zoey peers out, calling street names, watching endless scenery roll by and feeling sicker by the second. "Are you planning to do this all day? We haven't even had our breakfast yet," she complains finally. "I'm feeling sick. Besides, you know I should be eating with the pills I'm taking."

"It's impossible to get sick in this car," says Eli firmly but he finds a drive-through where he orders burgers, fries and shakes for two. "You spill any sauce on this upholstery and we're both dead," he warns.

Zoey unwraps her meal. "I don't see why we don't go in someplace decent," she says, eyeing the precooked meal distastefully. "It's ridiculous! Here we are in a million-dollar sports car chowing down on takeout sawdust! Speaking of, are you cooking at your house these days?"

Eli shakes his head, chewing rapidly. "I still use your kitchen. I hope that's cool with you."

"As long as you don't bring any babes in there. It is my house."

"No babes, just Jer."

"How is Jerry?"

"The same, you know." He scrubs his hands and mouth with balled-up paper napkins and sets them carefully on the tray. "He said I should bring you back. What time do you have to be at work?"

She glances at her wrist. "About two hours."

"Let's go to Stanley Park." He drives by the trash container to dispose of garbage from their meal, then Zoey directs him through the downtown streets to the park entrance.

"You have to stop," she says. "I'm not kidding El, I feel really sick."

He pulls off the road and they leave the pristine car gleaming richly under sunshine. Zoey clasps his hand as they pass by totem poles and thick-trunked trees.

"I've been meaning to ask," he says in awhile, "what you meant the other day."

"About what?" she asks.

"That thing you said about your being frigid."

"You said that, not me."

"About your being queer then."

"I didn't say I was, I said I thought I might be."

"Same thing."

Zoey drops his hand. "No it's not."

"Don't get pissed!" says Eli. "Just answer me!"

"First tell me why you got so mad."

"Because you aren't like that. You're into guys."

"George has both. Boy and girlfriends."

"You see?" He throws up his hands. "That sort of shit just ticks me off! What guy in his right mind would put up with that?"

"It doesn't seem to bother George's boyfriend."

Eli snorts scornfully. "Then he's probably a faggot."

"I don't think so," Zoey says. "But I could be wrong. I don't know what I am anymore. Maybe I'm just confused by all the changes in my life."

"Okay, big deal, you're frigid. That doesn't make you a dyke. Or bi, or whatever the hell these world-class-city trendoids call it." He glances at his watch and then uneasily back to where they left the Jag. "I think we should get going now," he says. "We don't want to have you late for work."

When Zoey arrives at the theatre, George is already in the box office counting out the float. "How was your day?" she asks cheerfully.

Zoey shrugs and slings her leather jacket across the counter top. "We rented this obscenely expensive car and walked around the park a bit. No big deal."

"Are you alright?" asks George. "You don't look well."

"I get carsick," Zoey says. "Thank god it's only one more day."

"You're not going back with him?"

"That was his idea, not mine." One by one, Zoey cracks her knuckles. "He can't have his own way about every stinking thing."

George exhales and concentrates on arranging bills.

When Zoey's done her shift, Eli is waiting for her in the XK8. "I was nervous about driving," he says, "so I left her at the parkade and walked to Gastown." He tosses several plastic baggies across the seat. "There's a few pairs of earrings and some other shit in there. For you."

"What's for Lori?" she asks snidely.

"Don't go weird on me. I also got a book for you. It's poetry. I hope you like it."

"George wrote two books. They're in the library."

"Of poetry?" he asks, peering through the rain-stroked windshield.

"She calls them novels."

"I wrote a poem for you. It's in my suitcase; remind me to give it to you."

Back in their room he reads his little poem aloud. It's not great but at least it shows he's trying. He gave up writing after high school. They make love and he waits till afterwards, when she's cradled in his shoulder, to tell her. "Lori's pregnant," Eli says.

love letters

Eli,

I'm sitting here on George's bed (don't freak, she isn't in it) trying to figure this all out. I just can't believe it. First, your being here in Vancouver with me and second, Lori's being pregnant. You don't know how much it hurts me, especially after what I've been through this year. I know you blame me for what happened but it's over now with no one but us the wiser and what's done is done.

I guess I've lost you forever because even though you say you want me back, I don't think you really mean it. I think you'd be happier without me fucking with your perfect normal life. Not having me around will just take a little getting used to. But you obviously don't love me and now that she is pregnant you wouldn't leave her anyway. Believe it or not, I'm actually starting to think I deserve more than what you give me. Naturally though, I still love you.

yours,

Zoey.

crumpled ball

She lets herself back into the room where Eli has slept alone all night most likely without even noticing that she was gone. She left here after midnight and now dawn strokes the sky. Stealthily she sits on the bed beside him. Quietly she removes her boots. Strips her clothing from her body. Takes her place beside him. The poem he wrote for her is an angry crumpled ball upon the bedside table. She wants to read the words again to see if there's anything she might have missed, but the unfolding would be too loud. Her mouth is gritty; she should brush her teeth but won't. For fear of waking Eli. Instead she makes a semicircle around his body where she always fits so perfectly and pretty soon she too is sleeping. When his soft words trickle over her she smiles and dozes on. Much later she awakens to his gentle brushing fingers.

"Morning babe," he says softly. "You can't sleep all day."

She yawns and leads his circling fingers to her breast. "Touch me there," she says sleepily.

"I'm lost without you in my life," he whispers, feathering her nipple. "Without you, I forget who I am."

She slides her hand on him the way she knows he likes it. "I can't go on this way," she says. "It hurts too much."

"You mean because she's pregnant?"

"That's part of it."

His forehead wrinkles. "There's nothing I can do," he says helplessly.

"You could leave her."

"You know I can't do that."

She looks at the eager flesh stirring in her hand. "Nothing else leaps to mind," she says.

"I can't think while you're doing that."

"Should I stop?"

He shakes his head. "Please don't," he says.

She spits his come onto his belly. It's softer now than it used to be. If he's not careful, it will turn to fat. Too much good food, a soft life and ambition wasted. Too much of all the things money and security can offer. She rests on the familiar chest. At least now she knows it's not the fucking with him she will miss.

He sifts her hair through his fingers. "So," he says at last. "What now?"

"You leave."

"You could come too."

"No I can't. I promised George I'd give her proper notice."

"You don't care about her stupid gofer job." Eli sniffs. "That's just an excuse."

Zoey twists her tongue around his nipple. "I tell you what," she says sweetly. "When you figure out what you want from me, let me know. Then I can decide if it's what I want too."

"How do you mean, what I want?"

"If you want me to be your forever-mistress or a short-term lover or a friend who happens to appreciate your cooking."

Eli pushes her away. "And while I'm doing that, would you be screwing other people?"

"You mean the way you do?"

"I don't like your being with other guys."

"And I don't like your being with your wife. What time is your flight?"

"Three-ten. But first I have to bring back the car."

"So get packed."

"Can't we resolve this?"

"The way I see it, we already have."

While he is in the shower Zoey tucks her letter into a suitcase pocket for him to find at home when he unpacks. They return the car, Eli gets his deposit charged back to his Gold Card, then they catch a cab out to the airport. "I still haven't decided," he says, "if I should order the XK8 now or hold out for the XJR in the fall. But whichever, it'll definitely be red."

"It's so obscene," says Zoey. "You could feed a huge family for ten years on that amount of money."

"It's a symbol," Eli says. "It's important. My business is doing great. And if I want to be successful, I have to look prosperous. Clothing makes the man, as the saying goes."

"Where will you put the diapers and the baby and the wipe-its?" asks Zoey edgily. "You'll get Pablum spittle on the upholstery. Besides, there isn't room for three."

"Lori drives the hatchback," Eli says. "It's not an issue."

"So the dumpy Honda is for the baby and the wife, and the classy sports car is just for you?"

"That's the way it's done," he says firmly. "Only you would think there's something wrong with it."

At the airport they scramble through construction zones trying to locate Canadian departures. Finally they find his gate and then they're out of time. One quick kiss and he is gone.

cultural exchanges

"I want you to come to New York with me." Jean Paul breaks a dinner roll and reaches for the butter.

George feathers a napkin across her lips. "When?"

"The Gallery is featuring a show of contemporary Canadian painters as part of a cultural exchange. The opening's next Friday. I have the impression Nancy Rider and myself are supposed to be providing some kind of weird politically correct version of a west coast dichotomy."

"Nancy's going?"

"Don't forget, you still owe me for Paris."

"I think this fixation of yours on my so-called debts is unhealthy."

"Come on," he wheedles. "Zoey can handle the theatre for a day and you deserve a break."

"Well . . ." says George. "Alright. I'll go if I can arrange it."

On Friday during brunch in the hotel suite she scans the New York papers while Jean Paul paces, anxious with his usual pre-show jitters. He frets about his clothing, hair and the paintings he's arranged to show and tells her sordid bitter tales about some sculptor from the Maritimes who should be hanged although hanging is much too good for him. George sifts through theatre listings even though there's no chance of getting tickets at this late date.

"You're not paying attention!" he accuses.

She does not look up. "I've heard every single thing you've said."

"Prove it."

"You can't decide between the navy and the black and you don't think you should wear a tie. And you're pissed about that sculptor Brian or whatever his name is."

"Bruce, his name is Bruce. You see, you weren't listening. He destroyed my painting because he didn't like the way they displayed his *art*. My painting mind you, not even his own work, without apology. What are you reading in all those papers?"

"I was hoping to find a show we might still get tickets to."

"It's much too late for tickets. Next time plan ahead."

"Next time invite me in advance. Then the trip wouldn't be a total waste."

His voice rises. "You consider it a waste to be supportive of my work?"

George sets her mug down angrily. "I know you're nervous, but cut the crap! Everything will be just fine, you'll see. The critics adore you. Remember Paris?"

"That's different. This is New York! Who can tell what these critics think, if they think at all. I'm asking you to stay away from Nancy. I get so tense and you know what she's like."

"Did you bring your tranquillisers?"

"I was hoping I would not resort. I was truly hoping that."

"Just ten milligrams," she soothes. "It'll help to ease your tension."

Nancy has been busy and by the time George and Jean Paul arrive it seems she's intimate with everyone. "Sweetie!" she crows, latching onto George. "I've been expecting you!" Leaving Jean Paul behind, she glides her through the rash of nerve-wracked displaced Canadians. With her trademark easy-access leather micro-mini, lacy thigh-high stockings, deep cleavage and obvious bad girl piercings and tattoos a magnet for everything she craves, she makes the breezy introductions that are her stock-in-trade. "Rexxie baby, this is George. Rex here is with the *Times*. And where has that man of yours gotten to? Rexxie, you absolutely must meet Jean Paul." She gestures. "These oils you've been ogling are his. He's just returned from Paris with fabulous reviews. Georgie, am I right?"

"Absolutely."

"Although frankly I find his work slightly retro . . ."

George rushes to drag Jean Paul from the bar. "Come on! Nancy's got a live one! A critic for the *Times*!"

Her hand by now planted firmly on the critic's bum, Nancy beams. "Ah, there you are! Rexxie, meet Jean Paul, the author of those terrific oils."

The two men launch into tense talk of paint, canvas and realism while Nancy links arms with George. "What a waste!" she moans when they are out of earshot. "Gay. Fantastic buns for spanking, did you notice?"

"That's a stunning outfit, darling."

"Isn't it? You know how much I love this city! We have to shop." She nods at nearly everyone they pass while George as her appendage smiles and shakes frantically thrust hands from those who think everyone is pivotal to their career. She tries to memorise names and faces to introduce Jean Paul to later. Nancy probably has fucked them all. "Of course you've heard of Lazarus." Nancy lifts a drink from a passing tray.

"Maybe; I'm not sure. Refresh my memory."

"Famous masochist, he makes his living at it. Performance art that consists of public mutilation, piercing, scarring; he hammers his dick to boards, dangles heavy metal objects from it, that sort of thing. Scar tissue is his life. It's all the rage; he's making scads of money. Want to meet him?"

"Mutilation as performance art?" George shudders. "I'd rather not shake his hand. Maybe you could point him out."

"He's kind of hard to find. He's really short. By the way, what they say about short men, it's all true you know."

"Hitler was short."

"Precisely! There, you see? Over there, behind that column. He's here to promote his book. You're sure you don't want to meet him?"

"I think not."

"Then come out with me; keep me company while I smoke." Nancy leads her through the tall glass doors. She flips open a platinum case, removes a slender cigarillo and snaps her lighter to it. "What he does isn't all that bizarre, you know."

She exhales a thin stream of dusty smoke which George longs to suck straight from her coral mouth. Instead she gazes out at the sparkling city.

"Body scarring represents the artistic tradition of a lot of aborigines," she continues. "Tattooing and piercing were used to create art long before pigment and papyrus. We colonialists have never had much of value to contribute at the best of times so we borrow from other cultures. I call it misappropriation. But despite your lofty beliefs about the purity of art, doing mutilation for pay isn't all that evil. I say if you get off on it, that's a bonus." She leans across the ornate railing to flick an ash, giving George a sidelong glance. A small grin rubs her mouth. "My body, their money. I've considered doing it myself."

"Don't you dare! Don't you even think about it! You'd never ever get away with it! Three reasons. One, because you're female. Two, because you are Canadian. And third, you enjoy your private mutilation far too much to share it with the public."

"I could make those first two work for me." Nancy giggles. "Being Canadian and a woman, I could become obscenely famous for it! Scarring myself in public as an established artist? I'd be the first. Really, really, really fucking famous! Think about it!"

George groans. "It would just be such a waste! After all these years of paying your dues! All the time you've spent establishing your credibility! You've worked too hard to be invited to shows like this. You have independence with respect. And you'd give it all up for some cheap party trick? I don't give a flying fuck about the cultology of art, on you it would look cheap. This Lazarus, it's probably the only thing he can do. He's never made it in the mainstream like you have. No one would ever take you seriously again. It would be artistic suicide."

"Ah-ha!" Nancy snaps her fingers. "Public suicide! Now there's a thought! Don't sneer; suicide has made a lot of artists wealthy. Once they're dead, their prices shoot right through the stratosphere."

"Too bad they're dead," George mutters. "So they can't benefit from it. But I suppose you've already considered that petty inconvenience."

"Writers too," says Nancy, flicking ash. "How many can you name offhand whose work became priceless after death? Just offhand? Twenty, thirty, fifty?"

"Not Canadians," protests George. "Not one single Canadian. Zero. Zilch. We kill ourselves with far less drama anyway, most of us. We do it through poverty, naïveté and drunkenness, and our prices don't nudge the ceiling let alone the stratosphere. What about your father; his death didn't exactly make you wealthy, did it?"

"My father!" Nancy snorts. "He never had a lick of talent to begin with! By the way, speaking of family, how's that sick kid of yours?"

"Pardon?"

"The one you threw me out for the other night."

"Oh. Zoey."

Nancy snaps her fingers. "Zoey, that's it! Sweet Cheeks. How is she?"

"She's looking after the theatre while I'm gone."

"So she works for you! My precious, are you diddling your employee?"

"That is none of your business."

"So you are! Is she as good as me? Stupid question, of course she's not! No one is. Besides, she's just a baby, she has a lot to learn. I never knew you were into infant skin but I, for one, would dearly love to have a bite. Are you absolutely certain you can't spare a teeny nibble?"

George glares. "Nance, I'm warning you, back off! I'm only here for JP's sake. I shouldn't even be talking to you. And I definitely should not be taking any of your bullshit."

"Ooooh!" Nancy shivers gleefully. She wraps her arm around George's waist and hugs her close. "I just adore your ultimatums! Let me tell you hon, there's this private room upstairs . . ."

"I'll just bet there is! You've probably made it there with everyone but me."

Nancy's black eyes glisten. "It's really rank down here," she coaxes, her voice rough. "Come up with me. I know you want to, you may as well admit it. For old times' sake if nothing else." George smells the musky scent of pussy Nancy dabs behind each earlobe and through the doors the stifling heat of humans wound up too tight and close together. Rex and Jean Paul are still off rubbing egos in a corner. "Follow me," purrs Nancy, knowing she has won.

Upstairs the floor is concrete. Watery blue light reflects eerily on Nancy's skin, waxy white and corpselike. She leans against the wall of stone, lazily tugging up her skirt. Thrusts her tattooed pelvis toward George who drops weakly to her knees. Hypnotised by music pounding from below and Nancy's throaty voice above, she sinks her face in what is being offered. Then someone slithers down beside her. "Did you invite this guy?" she growls.

"Of course," Nancy says serenely. "He can stay."

George stands up, steps back, while deep inside a foul wedge of grief or pain or anger or blind rage gains mass. This scene is too familiar, an audience gathering around her goddess, and then someone aims a camcorder at where Nancy kneels on concrete centre stage with Lazarus's metal-studded cock grinding into her. There is grunting. There is hot breath. There is red blood. It's what Nancy herself prefers, her own free choice. George knows she's been the bait again.

She finds Jean Paul huddled on a bench beside a potted palm, clutching a whiskey bottle to his chest. She pries it from him. "Not too bright, boy-o," she says scornfully. "On top of downers. Not too very smart at all."

pussy & perfume

A single lamp illuminates the storage room in which she crouches. No Georgie hunched over her computer, the office dark and empty. Zoey slept in on Friday morning and decided to stay late to make it up. Only she's lost track of time. When Carl the caretaker poked his head around the corner awhile ago and asked if she'd be leaving soon, she barely nodded. But now without his puttering, without George's clattering, without the phone ringing, with just the sound of her own breathing, of just one person in the occult twilight of the theatre, she shivers. Her knees crackle when she stands. Behind her is the stage, bare and black. The posters she has been unravelling for the past few hours, of shows staged here, threaten now to come to life. She finds the panel and throws the key to illuminate the platform and strides onto mid-stage. Holding an imaginary microphone she recites a poem, one of her own, to the plush red seats hidden beyond the light. The jangling of the phone startles her. It might be George calling from New York. She dashes down the hallway to the office, flipping up the light switch as she passes. "Zoey here," she gasps just before the machine answers.

"Hiya babe," Eli says. "Why are you still there?"

"Oh, it's you," says Zoey. "I slept in so I'm working late."

"Is George there?"

"Uh-uh. She's in New York for the weekend."

"I don't like your being all alone. Anything could happen. Anyone could walk right in."

"I can take care of myself! Besides, the doors are locked. Carl did it before he left."

"Don't you ever watch horror shows?"

"This is not a movie."

"There's serial killers in Vancouver."

"There's murderers in Roseville too."

He sniffs. "There hasn't been a murder here in more than fifty years."

"Then you're due for one. Why did you phone if you didn't think I'd be here?"

"To tell you there's an Air Canada flight leaving Vancouver for Winnipeg at eleven-forty your time and it isn't full, I checked. You've got two hours to get on the plane. I'll meet you at the airport."

"Stop it, El!" says Zoey angrily.

"Wait! Don't hang up! I've thought it through. What you are to me, I mean. You're my friend, my very special friend."

Zoey sighs. "Where is Lori at this minute, El?"

"What difference does that make?"

"I just want to know where she is right now."

"Alright, fine! I'll play your stupid game! As far as I know, she's at home."

"And where are you?"

"I'm at your house. I'm cooking dinner and you're invited. Hop on that plane!"

"Why should I?"

"I need you here to eat my food."

"I'm going to hang up now."

"No! Wait! Please! Just tell me what I should do."

"You should leave your wife."

"My wife is pregnant."

"There's your fucking answer, El!" Zoey slams down the receiver and grabs her jacket. The phone rings again and although she urges herself to keep going, she can't. "Hello," she says again.

"Zoey?"

"Yeah."

"Don't be mad."

"I'm not."

"I told you what you are to me. What more do you need?"

"Didn't you read my letter?"

"Which letter?"

"The one I put inside your suitcase when you were here."

"Jesus! You hid a fucking letter in my suitcase? Are you insane? Lori unpacked it."

"She unpacks for you?"

"Wives do that for their husbands. What was in that letter?"

"I don't remember word-for-word. But I think you'd better get your hands on it before she does." This time it's Eli who hangs up first. Zoey stands, still clutching the receiver. Then she digs out George's private address book from the desk and flips through quickly for a familiar name, a club that George has mentioned. It's Friday night. She's in a city all alone with not a soul she has to answer to. Build a new life for just herself, one that does not contain him, his snoopy sexist wife or their unborn baby either.

The place she has found is dimly lit, loud with drumming and the heavy scent of smoke and crammed-together sweaty bodies. Leather, lace and denim. Pussy and perfume. On the dance floor she creates herself a space. Strangers' hands wipe over and embrace her. *So this is how it's done* she thinks with some surprise. It is so easy to be touched. She shuts her eyes dizzy with the momentum of fingers on her skin that moves her into an inner sanctuary where women fondle one another's bodies. Her nostrils flare with woman-musk like dusty candle wax. She tugs down her shorts and spreads her legs and someone takes her just like that. She could dance like this all night.

sin

At dawn Zoey lets herself into George's. Some safe place is what she needs. Holding strangers has never been her thing. Until now her life has revolved around the same someone, someone who never wanted her enough. Maybe everything that's happened really is her fault. Maybe she is paying for her past sin now. She pours wine and pokes around the fridge for something sweet to fill her empty spaces, ice cream, cheesecake and chocolate pudding. She takes her booty to the window, looking out to where the mountains are, to where she could see them if it weren't raining. But it's always raining. What good is a view if you can never see it? She empties out the ice cream carton, then stuffs in pudding, cake, chips, sour cream, crunchy granola and then more wine. After she has consumed everything her mouth can handle she sticks her finger as far as it can go down her throat.

Jean Paul is hungover as sin and just as bitchy. Dramatically demanding coffee and hugging his head. "Why did you let me do this to myself?" he whines. "You're supposed to be taking care of me."

"You haven't put me on the payroll yet," says George. "When did what you choose to do to yourself become my responsibility?"

"Why did you go upstairs with her?"

"What do you mean?"

"You know what I mean. It makes me look like such an idiot. You were there with me."

"What makes you think I went with her?"

"For chrissake, I watched you do it! God only knows what you've picked up from her; she's fucked everyone else out here, no doubt without protection. I thought you were finished with her. Didn't you order coffee?"

George has lost all patience with his self-indulgence. "I've called down twice," she snaps. "Figure it out yourself. I'm going shopping." Meeting Nancy is so easy. Statuesque and gorgeous with attitude to match. Sometimes George thinks she does what she does just because she can and for no other reason, the script prewritten on her DNA. Nancy has spotted her so she doesn't have to wave or leap or resort to any other lunacy she could use to attract attention.

"Sweetie!" she calls out, swooping gracefully.

"I'm sorry I'm so late. I've been with JP all morning. He's sick and self-pitying."

"He's a fool." Nancy takes her hand. "And so are you my pet, for indulging his ego and his endless histrionics. Rexxie drooled all over him. He's convinced that he's a prophet with his nouveau-retro-this and post-retro-that. JP's the only one who got into the *Times* review. Being a retro-quaint-post-Canadian male is hot, I guess."

"What's old is new. Tell me why you hate JP."

"Why does he hate me?"

"That's just it, neither of you is talking."

"He hates me because you don't."

"Who says I don't?"

"You're here with me by choice, aren't you?" She squeezes George's arm, expertly ignoring whooping catcalls from a passing car of teenaged boys. "There's this incestuous navel-gazing clique of artists," she says. "It's inevitable that sooner or later we all piss off someone in it. And you can bet I've pissed off my share, your friend the retro-artist being one of them. Maybe it's because I don't pretend to like his work."

"Speaking of," says George. "I'm still pissed at you."

"Whatever for?"

"Last night. You used me."

Nancy bats her lashes coyly. "You know I'll make it up to you," she coos. "I always do."

George shivers with delight. The sun is shining, she is shopping in New York with Nancy on her best behaviour, oozing charm, how could she possibly stay angry? Their first stop is a trashy shop specialising in fetishwear featuring skin-tight spandex, splash-proof plastic and industrial rubber replete with incongruously girlish hooks and eyes, slits and push-up this and pull-down that with lots of fussy laces.

Nancy swoops around the store, scooping up an armful. "I'm trying these," she tells the bored attendant who yawns and gestures at a dressing room. "Georgie-girl, come in with me. I need your help." In the tiny booth she wriggles in and out of scanty undies while George watches, getting hot. "Lace me up," she orders, turning. "White is nice, don't you think? So virginal."

"Remind me to bite my tongue," says George.

"How is everything?" the attendant calls.

Slowly Nancy slides the curtain open. "That depends," she drawls, "on what you think. How's this?"

The woman exhales, suddenly awake. "Breathtaking!" she exclaims.

"Is it too small?" asks Nancy coyly. She reaches for the woman's hand and sets it on her bulging breast. "Tell me what you think."

"I think you have a perfect body."

Grinning, Nancy draws the curtain. "She felt my tits!" she whispers loudly.

"Behave yourself!" scolds George. "I'm on to you!"

"Are you kidding? You think we're here to buy cheesy panties? I can get those anywhere, anytime. We came in for a thrill. We can all have fun with this." Then preening Nancy cuts herself into as many pieces as she can, ass, breasts, pelvis, crotch and she is right, the fleeting glimpses of forbidden flesh, her brilliant tattoos and flashy piercings hold excitement for them all. The attendant's nipples poke stiffly through the soft fabric of her blouse, her tongue protrudes between flaming ruby lips, her breath is quick and forced and shallow. George's vulva aches, her clitoris throbs and even Nancy's skin is flushed.

When at last she's had enough she piles her booty high upon the counter and presses her Gold Card into the woman's hand. "I'm an artist," she says. "I'd love to do you sometime. Here's my number. You should call!" Then she swishes through the open door while George waits for her receipt and gathers up her purchases.

"I'm disappointed in you," she says outside to a giggling Nancy leaned against a lamp post.

"In me?" Nancy lifts her brows, amused. "This is the entire purpose of our trip. It's the only reason people like you hang out with me, to fulfil your fantasies, the ones you don't have the vulva for on your own. Why bother to pretend otherwise? You got to watch me strip, dress and flirt and she has fodder for wet dreams for months. She'll fantasise about posing naked for me, but she'll never call. I've given her the kind of perk for her jerky minimum wage job that can't be bought."

"Alright," says George. "You win. It's just that I was hoping for a little more, you know, personal involvement. Some private action."

"I perform, you watch," Nancy says flippantly, opening her cigarette case. "What's wrong with that? It all works out. Some people are performers and others are voyeurs. It makes the world go round."

"Your world maybe," George retorts. She seizes the lighter from Nancy's hand and touches gold flame to black paper.

"And which are you?" Nancy teases, sucking. "A watcher or a doer?"

"Jesus!" sputters George. "If you have to ask me that, you can carry your own damn parcels!"

The next shop she chooses is more upscale, silks and satins instead of lace and leather, and a frowning shopkeeper who looks like someone's frowzy Aunt Matilda. Wicked Nancy checks her out, nods approvingly to George, then moves rapidly about the store stuffing bits of glossy fabric into her hands. She pushes her ahead into the cubicle and swiftly pulls the curtain. "Okay," she mutters. "Here we go. And just remember that you asked for it." She sweeps her down onto the ornate three-legged chair, pushes apart her thighs and on her knees inserts herself between them. She licks her lips. "Mmmm! No panties. I like that in a woman I'm about to blow."

She slides in one sure finger, then another while George slips off her heels and presses her bare feet flat on either side of Nancy against the mirrored wall in which she can see every little thing reflected. She hears Matilda asking if they need her help. The curtain twitches. She sees the woman's scarlet nails tugging back the drapery, followed by pursed lips and tight eyes; George meets her disapproving gaze while defiantly she arches up her pelvis, opening her wet self a little wider, panting. The curtain falls. "She saw," she whispers hoarsely.

Nancy's throaty laughter bubbles on her skin. "Come on," she urges eagerly, taking clit between full lips she smoothly sucks, the inside of her mouth like velvet. "Just a little more. Come on now babe, come on . . ."

Coming against her teeth feels exactly like a death.

Nancy struts out triumphantly, wiping herself with lingerie before she plants it on the counter.

Matilda glowers. "Will you be taking this?"

Nancy smirks. "It's just so tacky! I would never wear it. Actually we just came in for a little . . ." she smacks her lips "snack." Head high she grabs for George and together they sail out onto a crowded sidewalk. "There!" she crows. "Don't say I never did you any favours!"

George grasps her hand. "I suppose I've forgiven you for using me last night."

"Of course you have!" Nancy is smug. "Only I haven't done a single fucking thing requiring forgiveness."

"I forgive you anyway," George replies.

Nancy laughs. "I'm ravenous! Let's find someplace good to eat."

In his hotel room, Jean Paul grips his cock tightly with his fist and finds another way to relieve his hangover.

And in Vancouver, with rain sliding down the window panes and over all her dreams, Zoey sleeps away the sin of guilt.

reviews

Jean Paul glances from the paper he is reading. "How was shopping?"
"I bought some panties." George throws her bag upon the bed. "You look better."
"I am. Here, look at this! A feature! A full-page spread!"
She leans over his shoulder. "I guess you have Nancy to thank for that."
"You smell fantastic."
"It's just sweat." She steps back. "From walking. I need a bath." She shuts herself in the bathroom and turns the water on full force. She removes her clothes and slides into the tub. Water brushes all the burning parts of her Nancy has recently caressed. She hugs the memory of tapered fingers dipping in and out with disapproving Matilda knowing just beyond the wispy curtain. Her knowing was the best. Nancy was the best. If only she could be certain she would never be used again, George would be ecstatic. She leans back and closes her eyes. Voluptuous, elegant and vampish, how could anyone resist? Nancy, with more talent in a single of her pulse points than Jean Paul has in his entire being.

Suddenly George wonders who it is she is pleasing now, these scant few hours since she was pleasing her. Because it is a fact with Nancy, being loved by just one person will never be enough. The fact with Nancy is the sharing and the blood-letting and those outraged fists of hers are equally as much a part of who she is as is who she was this morning. And although George herself does not agree with monogamy, the flaunting and the taunting and the blood are hard to take.

Jean Paul raps upon the bathroom door. "I'm leaving now," he calls. "I'll see you later at the Gallery."

"Okay," says George. "Have fun."

He is so easy. She knows exactly how he thinks and what he wants. His only unfulfilled desire is to marry, it's a simple simple little thing in exchange for which he will support her handsomely. He would continue to paint his critic-pleasing canvases and they'd grow old together side by side, the successful artist and his writer-woman. The security of this pledge is as beguiling as heroin. Of course she could be satisfied! It would be the end of all her worries. He says he will accept her sexual diversions. As long as they are with the Zoeys of the world, a fling for her and a fantasy for him, but whatever would he do with Nancy? Although he has promised freedom, George suspects there is a no-Nancy clause somewhere in that marriage contract he has been scratching out.

She pulls the plug and rises from the tub. She rubs her hair, wraps herself with a towel, glances briefly at the paper open to Rex's bloated feature all about Jean Paul, sags into bed and, in a moment, is asleep.

sacred temple

Zoey drags herself from bed at three o'clock in the afternoon. Avoiding her reflection in the bathroom mirror, she brushes her teeth. She drank too much last night. Before, after and during the sport of brushing bodies with strangers. Evidence of her impromptu feast is scattered all about but at least she's left herself a box of cornflakes. She finds it hidden at the back of a kitchen shelf; it's more than she deserves. The wax packing is still sealed; she slashes it open with a Henckels. Dumb luck like finding this boxful of cereal has dogged her all her stupid life. So what they had to move to hicktown when she was eight, leaving all the friends she ever had and her only known home, so what? If they hadn't, she would not have met Elijah. So what her mother's dead, at least she had one for awhile. So what her dad left when she was newly born, big deal! Lots of kids don't have dads at all and those who do are often abused or ignored, there's more than enough horror stories to convince her that having a dad is not the only way to go. So what about her baby, big deal. What difference does it make? There's just no fucking point to wasting time moping over her dumb luck. She holds her life in her own two hands; the only way to go from here is up. The one problem she has to solve is deciding who she's going to be. Because who she's been till now is someone who belongs to Eli.

She sprinkles cornflakes into a thick bowl made most likely by some ex-lover-potter especially for George and added to her collection after the lover turned out bad. She lifts the bowl and sure enough there's a personal inscription scratched into the clay. She sets it down and checks the fridge for milk. Typical of George, Häagen Dazs in the freezer and skim milk in the fridge. Skim or cream? Lesbian or not? Maybe it is in her karma to attract these fuzzy-edges people. Like Eli who can't decide which he wants more, wife or lover, even though he pretends he has.

Zoey forces herself to chew every soggy mouthful fifty times. It's what she does to control the urge to binge. She's already bloated and besides there is no food in this apartment any more. Staring through the window at the never-ending fucking coastal rain. Maybe she should go back to the theatre; she forgot to turn the lights off scurrying out in such a hurry. The lights might start a fire and wouldn't that be great? George would return to a heap of ash. Wouldn't she be thrilled with Zoey's dumb luck then?

But she stays stuck upon the chair, gazing through the mist, carefully chewing cornflakes out of some former lover's crock. Can't remember how many times she came or with who, no idea how many mouths and fingers she welcomed in. But one thing she knows for absolutely certain now is that she is not frigid. That Eli is mistaken at least in this. Her mother's voice clear as prairie sky rolls across her mind. *Your body is a sacred temple.* Her final words upon the subject which she herself had followed to the letter. After Zoey's father there were no more men. As she grew older Zoey often wondered about her father and her mother. Did he beat her up, the way some do, or did he keep a mistress like Eli's dad? Why did he leave? Maybe it was her he did not want, a useless baby girl, an everlasting burden. Maybe it was personal. Maybe he didn't like the looks of her.

Mother took all the answers, if they existed, to the grave. Even though Zoey combed their house thoroughly from the wooden rafters to the concrete cellar she never found the slightest scrap, no diary or letter or even photograph from which she might sketch out answers. She's stuck with nothing, a space into which the story of a father might neatly fit. Adopted kids can go out and find a family if they really want. They run ads in papers, Zoey's read them, they hire private dicks, those adopted kids who believe they have a right to know. She should run an ad herself, but why? If he didn't want her then, chances are he wouldn't want her now, all grown and used up. Maybe, if he does exist, he would try to steal the money that is her security, a legacy Mother left for her alone. Any way she turns it over, she comes out the loser. Got enough loser-karma without deliberately adding more to it.

She carries the pottery to the sink and rinses it, sets it upside-down on the drainer. All she wants to do is crawl right back under George's heavy quilt to stay forever. She should clean up the mess she's made. She should replace the food she's eaten. Or maybe she should rent some videos. Get dressed and face the rain head-on. Don one of Georgie's zillion funky hats and walk up the hill to the rental store. Videos would keep her from wandering around to let her body get her into trouble, and it would also take her mind off calling Eli to tell him every stupid thing she's done which is what she usually does when she feels lost or scared. *Fuck you,* she thinks, *just fuck you Mister Froese and that dappled horse you rode in on. Get on with your pregnant wife, your cheating dad, your position on town council, your fucking import, your orderly decided life. I'll take care of mine myself.*

trouble

Jean Paul as usual is morose coming down from a show. He and George have ceased speaking so it is a sullen ride from the airport to her building. He doesn't even help with luggage, he stops and waits for her to get it from the trunk. Fine, that's fine, all she wants is to wash off New York soot and drain away the weekend. She checks her messages. Nothing more than Smitty's husky reminder to bring her little friend in for a follow-up and perhaps George would like to go for drinks sometime? The kitchen is spotless, the dishwasher empty, the garbage has been taken out and there are groceries on the shelves she doesn't recognise. On the bed, clean sheets, but no sign of Zoey. Whatever was she hiding?

Zoey sits cross-legged on her cot circling apartment ads. The cost of housing is incredible, Eli would go mad. To call all these places from a pay phone she'd need a mess of quarters. Maybe she can find a private phone to use.

Jean Paul goes straight to bed. He has done his best at what he does, put out product and let the consumers dictate its value with their wallets. That's how art should be judged, with cold hard cash, although rave reviews can't hurt either. He is relieved to have escaped the PR mill for now. He tries to relax but when he shuts his eyes what he sees is endless Nancy, a cannibal with insatiable appetite foisting herself wide open on the world, George kneeling like a lap-dog at her feet with Lazarus hunched down like the greedy rat he is beside. Their pantomime was punched into his gut when he followed them upstairs at the opening. It should have been his weekend; George was supposed to be there for him.

Now he imagines that his penis is a crop he's bringing down on Nancy. The trouble with his fantasy is that instead of begging him to stop, she sneers *harder harder harder you're supposed to be the man.* She lures him damp-lipped into his bleakest fearful corners. His ragged breath grows sharper until every part of him goes soft.

The jangling telephone awakens him. He juggles it to find his ear. "Hello," he croaks. "Jean Paul speaking."

"It's me," Zoey sings. "I found you in the book. I hope you don't mind my calling you. I'm looking for a place to rent and I need to use your phone."

He squints at his illuminated clock. "What time is it?"

"A little after seven, why?"

"It feels like midnight. I've been dozing." He rubs his sticky skin. "Why not go to George's place?"

"I called but there's no answer. So, can I come over?"

"Of course. Oh, and could you pick up some milk? Two percent."

"Okey-dokey. Is your address in the phone book right?"

After giving her directions, he replaces the receiver. Gets up. Splashes icy water on his face. Scrambles through kitchen shelves and his refrigerator. Pasta, spinach and cheeses, he can concoct a decent meal. Dinner decided, he waits out on the stoop and in awhile he spots the slender girl round the corner across the street. He calls out and she stops, looks around, then waves before crossing over.

"There you are! Oh good, I thought I might be lost." She holds up a carton. "I brought your milk."

"Thanks," he says. "Have you eaten yet?"

"I had a bowl of cornflakes earlier. Actually, this morning."

"Then I'll make us dinner. How does garlic-spinach sauce with pasta sound?" He stands and opens up the door for her.

Inside, she slips off her sandals and sets them neatly on the mat. "Anything is fine with me as long as I don't have to cook it. Except for clams, I'm allergic." She pulls out the classifieds from her pack. "I'm looking at apartments; that's why I need to use your phone. Where can I park myself?"

"Right there is fine." He points to the couch and hands her the cord-

85

less. "But if you're looking for a place to live, I have an idea. Why not move in here? There's a room downstairs with an en suite bath. I don't use it except for guests. And half the time I'm out of town; it would be handy to have someone here to keep an eye on the place. You'd be doing me a favour."

"I don't know . . ." Zoey grins. "Georgie might not like it."

Jean Paul shrugs. "It's just a thought. Mull it over. Meanwhile, I'll start dinner."

Zoey spreads her papers on the coffee table. "Me and guys who cook," she says. "Elijah, he could be a chef if he wanted but instead he designs kitchens for other people to cook in. It's his wasted dream. Stupid, huh?"

"Elijah who?" Jean Paul calls over the butcher block partition.

She presses seven digits on the cordless. "My former boss."

"The guy who came out here? The boyfriend?"

"Not 'the boyfriend'!" says Zoey scornfully. "Just some guy, some married guy I happen to know. A married guy who has a wife with a baby on the way."

"I could swear George told me he's your boyfriend. Owns a Porsche?"

"Shit, no answer. Where is 879?"

"Timbuktu," he says. "Believe me, you don't want to live there." He tosses twelve whole cloves into a buttered saucepan. "I sure hope that you like garlic!"

"I love it! Oh hi. I'm phoning about the one-bedroom you've got advertised in the paper?"

Jean Paul listens while pouring pasta into boiling salted water, adding a dollop of extra-virgin olive oil. In fifteen minutes he has steaming dinner on the table.

Zoey unfolds her napkin and lays it on her lap. "This sure smells great! What's it called?" she asks, lifting her fork.

"Pasta. You know, noodles."

She eats with complete concentration, setting down her fork and knife after every bite and chewing slowly. When her plate is clear she carries it to the sink. "Thanks for dinner," she says. "It was really good."

"Would you like dessert now?"

"Actually I'd prefer a cup of coffee. And have you got an ashtray?"

Jean Paul gets up, scoops beans into the grinder and presses down the lid. "I think it's by the sofa," he calls above the noise.

Zoey sits down on the couch, sets her feet on the coffee table and lights a cigarette. "Where would I sleep?"

"Excuse me?"

"I mean if I moved in here."

"Downstairs. There's a bedroom with a bath."

"How much would you charge me?"

"Nothing."

"I said how much?"

"I don't want your money."

"I couldn't stay for free," she says. "It wouldn't look right."

"To whom?"

"To me. How about three-fifty?"

"You really ought to see it before making a decision," he says, gesturing. "The basement is through that door." While she is downstairs he fills the creamer and the sugar bowl, pushing aside her papers for the coffee tray. "Well?" he asks when she returns.

"Has anyone ever lived down there before?"

"No. Only guests."

"Can I share your TV and stereo and stuff, or should I buy my own?"

"You can use whatever of mine you need."

"Neat." She grins. "I think it could work out. By the way, how was it in New York?"

"New York was the same as always. Hot as hell."

"Did they like your paintings?"

"I got excellent reviews."

"Don't you ever wear a shirt?"

"Why? Does skin bother you?"

"I don't know." Zoey shrugs. "Skin is cool I guess, I'm just not used to seeing so much of it on other people. Man! Those boxers are something else."

"Something else, how? Too long? Too baggy? Uncool or what?"

"They're alright, just weird. Are you gay?"

"Pardon me?"

"Hey, don't bite my head off! It's an innocent little question."

"I am utterly and religiously straight! As a fucking arrow."

"So if I lived here, would we have to fuck?"

"No."

"Never?"

"Absolutely not! I am totally in love with George. And I have a one-track mind about that sort of thing."

"Okay!" Zoey laughs. "Then it's a deal. Let's do it! Three-fifty a month, can I move in tonight?"

Einstein's tattered bathrobe

She still has not accumulated much, her things fit easily into the same two bags she brought out from Manitoba. She bids farewell to her landlady and then helps Jean Paul set them into the trunk of his Jaguar.

"Welcome home," he tells her at the doorway of her new room. "I'll leave you to get settled."

She flops onto the waterbed, hers now. His paintings, most likely those not good enough to sell, adorn the walls. They are dark and heavy. She prefers Nancy's. Maybe she could buy one for herself; George could tell her how to go about it. Or maybe she would have to sleep with Nancy first. She might even enjoy doing it. She rests her hand on her pubic bone and wonders what George will think about her living here. Then she thinks about everyone she's ever needed who has in one way or another abandoned her. It's not a long list, but it is a list nonetheless. She gets up to unpack, storing her belongings in a few drawers while above the floorboards creak. Then Jean Paul calls her for dessert.

He wears an ancient tattered bathrobe, the kind every guy gets from his grandma, its rope-tie frayed, plaid patches faded. On his feet, well-worn moccasins, and his silver hair is blown out like Einstein's. Dessert is liquid chocolate drizzled over fresh whole strawberries, black cherries, blueberries, kiwi slices and rich clotted cream. Cautiously she lifts her spoon. Tells herself that she is safe here with this old man.

fidelity

Dearest El,

So did Lori find my letter? I'm sorry, maybe it was stupid but it honestly never occurred to me that you wouldn't unpack your own suitcase. I guess there are a lot of things about being married that I will never understand.

Hey, I've got my own place now! I'm renting it from George's boyfriend Jean Paul. He's a famous artist and I also think he might be rich. The house overlooks the ocean and is a short walk from the beach. I'm staying in the basement, it's one bedroom with a bath and we share the kitchen. He's a cook like you but don't worry, he's an old guy so nothing else is going on. Although why would it matter? You're obviously doing it with Lori or else how did she get pregnant? So obviously I don't owe you any explanations, not even being faithful when you get right down to it because you sure aren't!

I won't bother to ask you to write back and you can't call me here because I haven't got a phone yet. There's no point in giving you this address because you don't write anyway so what's the difference where I live? Anyway I hope everything is cool with you. Say hi to Jerry from me.

with love, Zoey

paper clips

Zoey breezes into work on a sunny Monday morning and plows smack-dab into her boss. "Georgie!" she howls, throwing out her arms. "Welcome back! Guess what? I'm no longer homeless!"

George scowls and thrusts the stack of paper she is carrying into Zoey's hands. "Here," she says. "Take this. Maybe you can figure out what to do with it. Why were the stage lights left on all weekend?"

"I'm really sorry. I was in such a rush to leave that I just forgot."

"Well. Turn them off and don't let it happen again."

While Zoey watches open-mouthed, George spins on her heels, strides into her office and slams the door. Zoey sighs and hauls herself backstage where she switches off the offending lights. At least there was no fire, her fears unfounded once again. Imagine thinking lights could cause a fire, even left on over a weekend! Probably the worst that could happen would be that they'd burn out. George's snub gives her that edgy time-to-move-on pang, the anxious churning in her belly that she knows so well. What did she do wrong? She crouches down to work. She's sure she replaced all the food she ate, did she leave lights on in the apartment too? Quickly she stands, sprints down the hall and breathlessly knocks on the office door.

"Come in," her boss says tonelessly. Slouched across her desk she looks like reheated leftovers. Like Jean Paul last night in his tattered bathrobe, George suddenly seems much older.

Zoey clears her throat. "I need those filing cabinets now. If I can use your car, I can go to the office supplies warehouse to get them. I know how to do it, don't worry. I furnished Eli's whole office when he and Jer first started out."

George raises her head and flops her hand. "He left an awful lot of messages for you this weekend, Elijah did."

Zoey shrugs. "What else is new? And you needn't worry about your car either. I'm a good driver."

"I trust you with my car." George pulls a credit card from her desk. "Go ahead. But please don't get any trendy colours, stick with black or white." Her voice softens. "We should talk. When you get back we'll go for coffee."

"Did I do something wrong?"

"We need to talk, that's all."

Zoey leaves her staring at Jean Paul's painting on the wall across from her desk. Easily she makes her way to the warehouse where she parks the Volvo in the customer parking lot. Inside it's cool and spacious with high steel-beamed ceilings. Zoey and her mom used to sneak away to stationery stores to cure their snowy-day depressions. Mom always managed to find some little thing the government refused to requisition for her office. She liked to sneak in non-regulation trinkets like the hot pink plastic paper clips that were her favourite. It was a small diversion, a tiny shared rebellion. These places remind Zoey of the times she felt the closest to her mother. Of being naughty giggling girls together playing hooky to buy forbidden paper clips.

Still, even here in office supply Nirvana, a train of fear rumbles through her stomach. Maybe George heard about her moving in with Jean Paul and maybe she's pissed about it. Or maybe she is jealous and just wants Zoey for herself. She did, after all, offer to check for an apartment in her own building. But she's the one who introduced Jean Paul to Zoey in the first place and besides she has never said anything remotely like *I need you* never mind *I love you* or *you belong to me*. Not that Zoey expects fine words or any promises at all. Eli has never made her a single promise, not in all these years.

She buys black cabinets, two dozen sturdy storage boxes and file folders with rainbow-coloured tabs. Then for fun she checks out laptop prices and CD-ROMs and bookshelves. She pays for the purchases with

George's card. A guy around her age with *Corey* on his name tag helps her load the car. The silver band on his left hand reminds her of Eli and she flirts shamelessly with him and then scolds herself the whole way back, nearly hitting a pedestrian on a crosswalk who shakes a fist at her. Anger can be dealt with; it's easy. Anger in, anger out. A simple equation everybody understands.

She slides the car keys across the desk to George who palms them. "Some kid named Corey phoned for you," she says. "He said he met you at the store."

"Oh yeah?" Zoey grins. "He's probably just checking to see if I got back okay. I told him I was new here. Did he leave a number?" Her boss gives her a Post-it note and Zoey reaches quickly for the phone.

George scowls. "I thought we had a date."

Zoey holds up two fingers. "Hi," she says. "Corey? Oh hi, it's me. Yeah, I just got back. I ran a red and almost killed someone, but otherwise . . . Yeah, sure, you too. Anytime!" She giggles. "You've got my number." Still grinning, she sashays out through the door George is holding open. At the café they get coffee, then sit outside where she can smoke.

"I've been thinking," George begins, stirring too much sugar into her mug.

"And?"

"I don't think we should be lovers anymore."

The tall woman who bumped into Zoey by the cash register lights a slender brown cigar and ogles her. "What did I do wrong?" she asks, staring back.

George snaps a wooden stir-stick in two. "It isn't you, it's me."

"Cool," says Zoey sharply. She wins the staring contest two times in succession.

George turns to see what she is looking at. "You like that?" she asks tightly.

"Yeah, I do," says Zoey. "So what? I didn't expect you and me to last a whole lifetime or anything but I'd sure like to know what I've done to piss you off."

93

"Oh please! It isn't anything like that. It's just that . . . Well, it might be as simple as you being too young for me. Or maybe it's that I'm too old for you. I just think it would be best to end it now, before either one of us gets too serious." She picks up a plastic straw and begins to twist it into a spring-like spiral between her fingers. "I saw Nancy in New York," she says finally.

"I thought you were there with Jean Paul."

"I was."

"But you 'saw' Nancy?"

"That's right."

"Are the two of you back together? Is that why you're breaking up with me?"

George threads the spiral around her fingers. "Not exactly," she admits.

"What then?"

"I just feel a need to simplify my life."

"That is so much bullshit!" says Zoey. The tall woman stands, nods and smiles pointedly at her. "I thought you didn't believe in monogamy. Are you dumping Jean Paul for Nancy too?"

"I am not dumping anyone! And I'm not dumping you for Nancy! That would just be foolish." George's voice is high. When she lifts her hands the spiral bounces to the table top.

"Whatever," Zoey says. That woman has great legs, she's young and she wears punky high-heeled sandals. Her right brow is pierced. She watches Zoey watch her smooth her hands along lithe calves. "I moved into his house last night. I tried to tell you earlier, but I don't think you heard."

George watches Zoey watch the stranger. "What did you just say?"

"I said I'm renting JP's basement."

"He never mentioned it."

"We didn't plan it. I just went over there to use his phone to call about apartments and one thing sort of led into another."

George snorts. "I'll bet it did!"

"Not the way you think!" retorts Zoey. "He never even touched me! It just seems like the perfect place for me right now. Besides, who are you to judge?"

The woman flexes a final time then struts over to their table where she stops and drops her card in front of Zoey. "You could call," she tells her crisply and strides away.

"Did you see that?" Zoey crows, picking up the card. "She hit on me!"

"This will happen," George says. "It's a small town. You're fresh meat."

"I'm not meat! Her name is Xandra; it says here she's a graphic artist."

"I've never heard of her."

"She can still exist even if you haven't heard of her. Maybe you don't know every stinking artist in this city after all. Does Jean Paul know about you and Nancy getting back together?"

George purses her lips. "We are *not* getting back together! I only spent some time with her. And for your information, in case you care, I'm not too keen on this living arrangement you two've cooked up. I don't think it's a good idea for either of you. He's old enough to be your father."

"And you're old enough to be my mother! So what? Who cares?" Quickly she gets up, stuffing Xandra's business card into her pocket. "Guess what? I don't need permission! This is still my life despite what everyone around me seems to think. I'm going for a walk! I've got some thinking of my own to do."

George sighs, watching Zoey walk away. She doesn't even know why she's called it off. Surely she is some kind of idiot if she imagines there might be a piece of Nancy in her future. After all, they've only had a single shopping spree, that circus set-up in the Gallery and a momentary thwarted coupling in her living room. Nothing serious. No more than diversion. But still Nancy has made too clear her fascination with Zoey who, for all intents and purposes, is a child, naïve and much too innocent for the damage that can be caused by the Nancys of this world.

frozen

George spends much of the afternoon replaying conversations she has had with her three lovers while noisily shuffling papers and slamming drawers to avoid dealing with her grant application. When she can't stall anymore she scrapes out a few academic-sounding phrases to describe her writing, then deletes them while the band of pain around her forehead tightens. Jean Paul calls. "I thought we weren't speaking," she says coolly.

"You thought wrong; that was a minor blip. Typical post-show stress, don't take it personally. I'd like to get together with you. Later?"

"I can't commit. I've got this application to get done."

"I say fuck it! Let me buy you dinner. By the by, my mother is coming into town this weekend. She says she'd like to see you."

"Tell her sure. I like your mother. Especially since we're not in any way related."

"Bear in mind that you don't need their money. All you have to do is say the word. The word is 'yes. Yes, I'll marry you Jean Paul.' It's so simple."

"I hear you have a roommate."

"Housemate," he corrects. "Since you keep rejecting my proposals, it seemed logical."

When she hangs up, Zoey is leaned against the door. "I'm leaving now," she says. "It's five o'clock."

"Alright." George turns back to the screen.

Zoey takes a step into the room. "Look," she says, spreading out her arms.

"What?"

"I've thought it over and it's okay with me if you don't want to fuck, I still want us to be friends. I've never really had a friend before so I'm not exactly sure how it works, but I don't think friends have the right to tell each other what to do. Like where they can or cannot live."

"That's fine," says George. "I'm sorry if I was harsh. It's just that there seems to be so much happening right now and I'm not even sure what I want. By the way, I keep forgetting to tell you, Smitty wants to see you for a check-up. Here's her card. Call her! I don't want you to get sick again and if you're having sex with men you're more susceptible to infection."

"Who said anything about sex with men?"

"What about Elijah?"

"That's over. But I get your point. I'll call the second I get home."

Zoey lets herself into Jean Paul's silent house. She hasn't seen leftovers in a fridge since hers, after Eli's cooking nights. She pulls out the first three containers she can get her hands on and a pot to make her special three-container meal. She sets the pot on the stove and turns on the element. Not much can go wrong with this kind of dinner.

When the food is hot she pours it out onto a hexagon-shaped plate, gets a fork and settles with it on the sofa. Finds a news channel on TV. They found the body of a transvestite in the trash bin beside the library downtown, the third transvestite murder of the summer. The cop spokeswoman says the killer is probably a john who likes it rough. A grainy copy of a high school photograph briefly fills the screen, followed by a shot of the body and the bin in which it was discovered, then a picture of the news reporter in front of the building saying something about a deeply troubled life. *Don't we all*, Zoey thinks. George's books are in that library and so is one of Jean Paul's paintings. She wonders what it would be like to find a hacked-up body. The way it's going, the odds are pretty good for everyone on earth to find at least one in their lifetime. They say a chill is sweeping through the Prairies from Alberta to Manitoba. She shivers. The phone rings. It's Jean Paul's mother Pearl, who asks Zoey to tell him to call her if he returns before she goes to bed at nine. Zoey flicks the channel to a Shania Twain music video and lies back.

Asleep on the leather couch, she dreams. A woman who her mind calls Nancy has carved precise patterns into George's body with a long sharp knife. Nancy is focussed, concentrated but immobile while George is still, dripping blood and grinning away with eyes as blank as ice. Beside them stands Jean Paul, frozen, a paintbrush poised weapon-like within his hands. Nothing moves. Their images stay caught until gradually she becomes aware of a cushion twisted beneath her elbow, the clicking of the answering machine, a pizza commercial. She runs her tongue around her teeth and swallows. Rubs her shoulder with a hand gone numb from lying on it.

A key turns the front door lock and Jean Paul enters noisily. "Oh good! You're home. I was hoping not to startle you."

Zoey scrubs her fist across her eyes. "I had the most bizarre dream just now. You were in it, and so was George. Nancy too."

He shudders. "An awesome trio."

"Nothing happened. You were all just there."

"That's the way it is."

"Have you talked to her?"

"To George?"

"Yeah. Did you tell her about my staying here?"

"I assumed you'd told her."

"I did." Zoey shakes her head. "God, that was one weird dream! Your mother wants you to call her back tonight if it's not past her bedtime. She sounded nice."

While he phones she fills a tumbler with cold milk. It coats her tongue and throat. The dream was manufactured by her mind, a silly early evening vision created out of the tangled insecurity left by George's kiss-off. She hasn't even met Nancy. She goes downstairs to shower, draping the full-length mirror beside the bathtub with a towel before she undresses so she won't have to see her naked self. Xandra's card and the Post-it with Corey's work number fall from her shorts onto the floor. She picks them up and sets them on her bedside table. Some-day she'll call them both.

necessities

Nancy mines the urban underground where any little thing is hers for the right price. Crossing boundaries, seeking out the secret places, tracking down those telltale silences in which forbidden pleasure happens. She paints a special stock and displays it privately at a hefty fee to only those who can afford her. Names it *ritual,* relying on the grapevine of the idle well-to-do with nothing but the gothic chic of deviance with which to entertain themselves. Their lust and boredom paper Nancy's bank account proving there are still ways for art to sell.

She is doing business where the money is. The thought of George ageing by the page, being fine and arty in poetic novelettes about important things that no one wants enough to pay for, makes her sick. She's been that route herself, staying pure and poor for the promise of paltry arts grants and the right showings for the right critics with her basic needs unmet. She has put her boot down on the purity of poverty. It's frailty that frightens Nancy. Vulnerability terrifies her beyond belief. It frightens her to death.

centrefold

This has been the longest, most dreary rain-filled month of Zoey's life. Eli still phones the theatre from his Roseville office and now they are pretending to be friends. He no longer begs or orders her to come home. Instead he tells her boring pointless stories about their new receptionist, Jerry's disastrous love life, their clients and his family. Mercifully he rarely mentions Lori. Since Zoey has no power and he has not enough desire they are each precisely where they've always been, clutching at each other's shadows with his wife and coming baby solid as a mountain in-between. *It would be easier if I knew you really loved her* Zoey writes but even as she writes she knows that it's not true. What's more true is it would be easier knowing he loved *her*. She doesn't send her letters anymore. Her usual mid-summer melancholy is tinged with guilt and grief wedged together tightly as a centrefold inside her. Thinking back to stolen moments in her mother's kitchen groping one another over Eli's gourmet meals for her to gag up later, Zoey decides to check up on her property. She makes a return trip airline reservation. She is flying home.

gentle fucking

Nancy calls her from New York. "I'm still here," she says. "I'm staying on. It's going well. I'm painting up a storm and selling too."

"Good for you," George says glumly. "I'm in application hell."

"Why bother with that bullshit? Just go ahead and do your work like me."

"You can't frame a story, hang it on a wall and expect someone to pay six figures for it."

"Find your own way to sell it. There are commercial ways to use your skill."

"Name one."

"Movies, advertising. Porn. Get to know your market and remember, sex sells."

"The days of cut to waves upon the shore and gentle fucking have long since passed; what they want is blood. That's your cup of tea, not mine."

"Writers are not the only ones who struggle." Nancy's voice is crisp. "And for every painter who can cull six figures for a work, there are thousands who cannot. You and your elitist attitude! Despite your ideals, it does take a certain amount of talent to realise your marketing potential. At the very least you could admit it isn't criminal to earn a living from your art."

"I never said it was!"

"You imply it all the time. But with all your virtuous ideals, you still grovel for their money. I tried to suck state dick for years; it got me nowhere. They would not have given me a grant if I'd crawled naked backwards over ground glass and impaled myself in front of them! But now look! My work is putting Canada on the map."

George stabs her pencil point into the paper she is doodling on. "Are you ever coming home?" she asks morosely.

"Ah my precious, are you missing me already?"

George's stomach lurches. "Yes," she says. "Yes, I am."

"How much?"

"Terribly."

Nancy giggles. "I could take you shopping."

George scratches a dollar symbol through the 'N' in Nancy. "In Vancouver?"

"How about in Frankfurt?"

"As in Germany?"

"I have a show there in October, all expenses paid. Nino's ironing out the creases in the contract as we speak. Me, with escort, to be fêted, wined and dined. You could come. You could even bring the child. Sweet Cheeks. And don't give a second thought to cost; I'll pay. For everything."

That night George sleeps fitfully and then awakens suddenly, writhing and in pain, blood staining sheets around her. It takes more than a simple minute to understand that she just got her period.

resurrection

The alarm at the crack of dawn wrenches Jean Paul from sleep. Lovingly he fondles his erection. Piss hard-ons, like death erections, are either the gods' little joke or an ultimate betrayal. The Pharaohs believed death erections were a blessing, Osiris's final opportunity to seize the womb of Isis. Not a joke at all but resurrection, a creation miracle.

He drips dry over the toilet bowl and steps into the shower. Normally he considers his greying hair a symbol of distinction, of having paid his dues, but today it just seems shameful. He has accomplished more than most but he still needs a wife. If only he could convince George to spend a year with him in Europe, the problem would be solved. He slips into forest green walking shorts, pours a cup of fresh-brewed coffee and skims the morning paper. Then he jogs the four blocks along the waterfront to his studio.

This afternoon he and George will meet his mother at the airport. He expects Pearl will move in with him when her time comes and it would help to have someone to look after her while he travels. A wife who writes, like George, would be ideal.

George feels like a child dwarfed in the back seat of the Jaguar listening to the two of them. Pearl says she wants to have a little lie-down before going out for dinner, Jean Paul says he planned to cook at home tonight and then they lapse into silence. George gazes through the window at estates along Granville, at other drivers gesturing with their cellphones, at taxis weaving in and out of nightmare traffic.

At his house he parks behind her shabby Volvo. "You take Mother in," he says, "while I get the luggage."

"Is Zoey home?" George asks, unlocking the door for Pearl who steps in marvelling.

"This fig tree of his must grow a foot a week!" she exclaims. "It's enormous! Pretty soon he'll have a forest."

George pokes her head through the basement doorway. "Zoey?" she shouts.

Jean Paul enters with his mother's bag. "She's probably asleep," he says. "She sleeps an awful lot."

"I'll just check," says George. She tiptoes down the stairwell. Upstairs Jean Paul helps his mother settle. Water taps squeal, a toilet flushes. The bedroom shades are drawn and the room is dark. George sets her hand upon a lump beneath the blanket which she assumes is Zoey and shakes it gently. "Sweetie! It's nearly time for dinner. You should get up."

"George?" asks the girl, emerging. "What are you doing here?"

"We just got back from the airport." She flicks on the bedside lamp. Zoey blinks and yawns. "What's his mother like?"

"Put on some clothes." George is stern. "Then we'll have a conversation."

"Why are you always ordering me to get dressed? I thought you liked to see me naked. Anyway, you'll have to get off my shirt if you want me to put it on so bad. I'm pretty sure you're sitting on it."

But instead of standing, George picks at the blanket. Upstairs Jean Paul and his mother chatter. Underneath this bedding is all of Zoey's tender musky skin. Without thinking, she runs her fingers down.

Zoey sticks out her tongue. "Stop it! That tickles! I thought you said we weren't doing this again. Didn't you just break up with me?"

George's voice is muffled by the comforter. "I'm pretty sure I've changed my mind."

"George?" Jean Paul calls down and then, after a moment, "Zoey!"

"Yeah?"

"Is George down there with you?"

George raises her head, finger to her lips. "Shhh," she hisses.

Zoey nods. "Yeah," she calls. "She's in the can."

"Will you be joining us for dinner?"

"I don't know. Yeah, sure, okay. What time?"

"I'd say half an hour."

"Alrighty then," says Zoey sweetly. "Just give us a shout."

The basement door closes and they hear his firm movements overhead.

"Atta girl," George says softly, combing Zoey's sweaty pussy. "And here is your reward for doing that so well."

There is not a thing on earth that could keep Zoey quiet now.

Triumphantly, George laughs. "Sometimes you just have to help yourself," she says.

speed of light

Zoey hates to fly. There is not a single thing about it that she likes. Not taking off, not being in the air, not looking out the windows, not landing. She hates the food they serve which she ends up picking at, eating because there's nothing else to do and chewing helps relieve the tension in her jaw. She hates airline movies. She hates airports with their line-ups and the staff who act like you should know their jobs as well as they do and treat you like a fool when you don't. She hates crowds and their perfumes and being captive inside any place. Airplanes are the worst because she knows she can't bail out when she's had enough, like the rides at circuses and country fairs designed to make you sick. Flying combines all the things she most despises into one neat usually avoidable package.

She's helped herself to Valium from Jean Paul's cabinet and she takes one in the taxi. It hasn't hit her by the time she's in the line of passengers waiting to check their luggage. She is so frightened she can't see straight, her mouth is dry and she feels dizzy so how will she know when the drugs kick in? A boy in line behind her makes idle conversation and tersely she rebuffs him.

Luggage checked, she heads for Gassy Jack's where she orders wine, lights a cigarette and takes another pill. People hang around in pairs talking, some are saying sad good-byes. On CBC she heard a panel of speculative fiction writers and futurists who all agreed that someday humans will travel at the speed of light and live on other planets or maybe even galaxies and will return to Earth for visits only. This planet will become a great big theme park, too polluted for actual habitation. Zoey hopes it won't happen in her lifetime and if there is reincarnation and she does return, she will not have the silly earth-bound fears she was born with this time. But they also said travel would take just an instant so maybe it would be bearable after all. At the speed of light there would not be time to notice line-ups and too many humans jammed unnaturally together in small spaces under glaring fluorescent light.

The cigarette she's smoking dries her mouth, but the drugs are starting to kick in. Why didn't she just take the train? Once she gets to Winnipeg International it will take another hour on the bus to get to Roseville.

detour

By take-off she is sedated and able to avoid the flight through sleep. When the plane lands in Winnipeg the steward nudges her awake and she stumbles off, buoyed up by other passengers also squeezing their way out. Hers is the second bag down the chute, she grabs it and hurries out to catch a Duffy's. "I'm going to the bus depot," she tells the cabbie. Peering through the windows at passing city landscape, past Eli's old apartment block on Ellice, the ninety-nine-cent video store and confectionery, past the University of Winnipeg. "On second thought," she tells the cabbie who is turning right at the Salvation Army, "how much would it cost for you to drive me all the way to Roseville?"

"Roseville," he says pensively. "I once knew someone from there."

"How much?"

"Let's see," he says, "it's about an hour's drive. How about a hundred? Up front. Before we leave the city."

She rifles through her wallet and passes him two fifties. "Let's go," she says crisply. When she left Vancouver it was mid-day. Here the sun is setting, the vast sky holding clouds and light in layers.

"Full moon," remarks the cabbie.

Zoey sighs and settles back. "Mind if I smoke in here?"

"Go ahead."

"In Vancouver you can't smoke anywhere, not even in the coffee shops or bars."

"You live out there?"

"Now I do but I grew up right here, in Roseville. I'm just out for a visit." They pass the Winnipeg Mint at the city's edge. The Trans-Canada is naked and stretched out with scrawny shrubs scratching the median.

Beside it run the train tracks. Eli doesn't know she's here. She lights another cigarette. In the west behind them the sun is inching down and up ahead the moon is fat and full and white. Tires hum along the glowing lines. Once in Eli's 911 they hurtled down this road at top speed; it felt like being in a shooting bullet.

The driver clears his throat. "Mind if I put in a tape?"

"Sure."

"It's an oldie."

"I don't mind." He slips in Audience's *House on the Hill*. It's been ages since Zoey last heard it. Eli used to use it to seduce new girls and it seems fitting to hear it now. At the *Welcome to Roseville* billboard, fear grabs her belly. "Turn right onto Main," she says.

"This takes me back," the driver says. "I knew this girl, well I guess we dated. We swam together on weekends at the Pan Am Pool and once I came out here to meet her family. Churchgoers, not my scene. Maybe you know her. Name's Christine. Christine Radamaker."

"Sorry." She shrugs.

"She's probably got kids older'n you by now. She just wasn't the type to leave; I was just a detour for her."

Zoey's stomach churns. "At the last set of lights, turn right."

"She would've gotten married and taken on her husband's name, that's the kinda girl she was. Odd how you lose track of people."

"Chances are," says Zoey tightly, "she's still here. That's the way it is in Roseville."

"Some leave. Look at you."

"Turn left at the church and left again the first street after." A dense hedge of lilac hides her mother's house from the street. Mom valued her privacy. The driver sets her luggage on the pavement and stands stretching out his kinks. "Thanks a lot." Zoey hands him an extra twenty.

"You don't have to," he protests, pocketing the bill. "But thanks. Stay cool man."

The grass is mowed and watered; red geraniums are in full bloom.

The house is lit and the back door stands open. The hair rises on her arms. "Mom?" she calls out softly without thinking. The screen door whispers shut behind her. She smells cooked food and there is Eli seated on a stool beside the kitchen counter.

"Holy fuck!" he shrieks, standing quickly. The stool clatters to the floor. "Where did you come from?"

Zoey laughs. "What's for dinner? Man, I'm starving!"

menopause & madness

"You're staying," announces Eli. "I refuse to let you go."

"I have a return ticket. I'm going back to work."

"You have a job here. All you have to do is say the word."

Zoey helps herself to extra sauce. Maybe it's the downers, but she doesn't feel like puking yet. "What's in this?" she asks.

"Chef's secret." He grins. "I'm not being cute; I honestly can't tell you. I combined recipes and then tossed in my own ingredients to see what would happen. I thought no one would be eating it except for me so if I fucked up it wouldn't matter. Jesus babe, I wish you had told me you were coming. I could've met you at the airport; I could've arranged to spend the night."

"Did Lori find my letter?"

"Nope," says Eli. "She hadn't gotten to it yet."

"I don't know about this marriage business, but you're a big boy now. You should do your own unpacking."

"She's got these ideas." Eli gathers up serving spoons and lays them in a stack. "Things a wife is supposed to do. She sees taking care of me as her job and if I tell her not to bother she gets upset."

"Sneaking around and making excuses, is that what being married is about?"

"It'll change," he says confidently. "Once the baby's born. That's what other guys tell me anyway, they say it's better when you start having kids. The more the merrier. They say it takes their minds off you."

"She could have a dozen, she still won't cut you any slack," says Zoey. "Can we talk about what was in my letter?"

"No. You'll probably assume that means that I don't care, but it's just

111

that I'm under all this pressure with my work and Lori and the baby and this shit that's happening with my mom."

"What shit with your mom?"

"She's in the hospital."

"What happened?"

"She just went crazy. Started ripping up the house and screaming for no reason and she wouldn't stop. They called me because my dad was out of town but even I couldn't calm her down. Man, she was wild! So they gave her a shot and hauled her off."

"Is she in Roseville General?"

"For now. They want to put her in a psych ward in Winnipeg."

"Who's taking care of Jen?"

"Jen's sixteen, she's old enough to take care of herself."

"How about your dad?"

"He's having the house redone. Finally. You know she's been after him to do renovations forever. I guess he figures it's the straw that broke her back. Mom won't let him see her."

"Any idea what really caused it?"

"I'm pretty sure it's the menopause. Dr. Schott agrees with me."

"Or maybe," says Zoey, rising to stack the dishes, "she finally found out about your father's mistress. Are we doing these together or do I get to do them all?"

"That shit can wait," says Eli. He arrests her with his arms, pressing his face against her breast. "There's no one in the world who smells like you," he whispers. "I'd know you anywhere. Blindfolded, deaf or dumb."

Zoey pulls away. "Maybe you'll get to spend a night before I leave."

"I won't ever let you go again," he insists.

Zoey doesn't answer him; there isn't any point. They always argue like little kids. Did not, did too, did not, did too and neither will let go. She has her return ticket and some Valium and nothing changes that. Besides, Jean Paul and George expect her back.

After he has left for Lori's, she inspects her house. There is no damage, he has done his looking-after job. She takes her bag to her mother's room where she sleeps when she is lonely or depressed or missing Mom, and all three are on her mind tonight. She digs out her toothbrush. Tomorrow she will look through her winter clothing and try to decide what to do with it. She'll walk around the town to see if anyone has noticed she has been away. Still, it's August and lots of people go on holiday or to cottages in the Whiteshell so no one is really missed until September. Or in her case, never. She lifts the spread from her mother's bed.

crunching seashells

"She didn't tell you where?" George is pacing back and forth across his living room rubbing her impatient hands together. "She must have given you a hint. Something, anything at all."

"I don't remember." Jean Paul shrugs. "Why don't you calm down? She told you she was taking the week off, she's got money, she isn't homeless or out hooking or shooting heroin. Give her a little credit for intelligence. She's seeking out experience."

"That's not good enough," snaps George. "I feel responsible. She's terribly naïve. What if she entrusts her life to a total stranger?"

"You mean the way she's done with us? This is your guilt, not reason, speaking."

"This is not guilt. This is a reasonable concern for an inexperienced child!"

"It isn't reasoned and Zoey is an adult. I think you feel guilty because you've been bedding someone who you think of as a child."

"It wasn't you who fucked her."

"Whatever."

George wheels on him. "What exactly does that mean? Did you fuck her?"

"Of course not." He lights his pipe. "But I would."

"She isn't ready for a man. You're too old for her and besides, she's still in love with Eli."

"How considerate of you to think of her well-being now."

Angrily George tugs on the doorknob. It always seems to stick during moments of high drama and it's sticking now. "When are you going to fix this fucking door?" she screams.

Calmly he reaches around her. "It's my fucking door," he says pleasantly, tapping his toe against it. "I'll fix it when and if I choose. You really should relax."

George storms out through the open door and stomps down the path. When he can no longer see her, he slips into his basement. The girl has left no clutter. He removes the towel covering the bathroom mirror and rehangs it neatly, then sits on the bed. One of his largest paintings has been taken down and is now leaned face-in against the wall. Zoey is fully capable of making her own decisions only George can't get that through her head. He climbs heavily back upstairs, dons his raincoat and leaves for his studio.

George walks along Kits Beach kicking at the pebbled sand and crunching seashells with her boots. The drizzle suits her mood. The beach is quiet except for a few diehards, joggers with their dogs and a handful of bored-stiff lifeguards. She took advantage of Zoey when she was vulnerable, sick and heartbroken. Most likely she has returned home to Roseville and her married swain and that will be the end of that. She chooses a log to sit upon to contemplate her options. With Zoey gone she is left with Jean Paul. When she wants a man he is always willing, available and safe, and even his repeated bribes of infinite security can be bewitching. But marriage? One afternoon with Nancy is worth a month with him. Maybe she'll do Frankfurt in October. There is no earthly reason why she shouldn't go.

satisfaction

Saturday morning Eli slips into the house before her eyes are open.
Shucks his clothes and crawls into her mother's bed. Quickly drains
himself and then lies heavily upon her. Barely awake she pushes him
aside and races to the toilet where she purges last night's dinner after
all. When she returns he is lying on his back sucking air in through his
mouth. *Lover of my life* she thinks, looking him over from head to toe.

She slips on a pair of jeans and a shirt and goes downstairs. Checks
her kitchen cupboards and the fridge. She left dry goods like crackers,
breakfast cereal, tins of soup and salmon, the food she feeds herself. Not
these clams to which she is allergic, not these herbs and spices she
barely knows exist. She resents them all, especially the clams. She asked
him to be caretaker, not to build himself another home. He has too
many homes already, he has his home with Lori, with his parents and
with Jerry when he chooses and now he has helped himself to hers as
well. She climbs back up the stairs to where he is snoring. "Eli!" she says
loudly in his ear. "Wake up! I have to talk to you."

He groans. "What now?"

"Why are you always sleeping when you are with me?"

"I got up early on a Saturday so that I could be with you. So sue me,
I'm tired."

"You got up early so you could fuck me. The only thing I got out of it
was woken up. If it doesn't matter to you if I enjoy myself or not, what's
the point?"

"Come here," he coaxes, patting at the pillow. "Lie down with me."

"Why should I?" Zoey asks impatiently.

"So we can have that talk you wanted," Eli answers smugly. Stiffly

Zoey sets down her head and Eli pats it gently. "That's much better," he says soothingly. "Now tell me babe, what's this all about? You think I don't care enough about you, is that it?"

"That's part of it," Zoey says, biting down her anger.

"I'm just not the kind of guy who talks about my feelings. I'm here with you; isn't that enough?"

She snorts. "I'd have to be really dumb to fall for that old line."

"Don't you worry! I know you aren't dumb." Playfully he tussles her hair. "Is that all you wanted to talk about?"

"There's this other thing." She hesitates. "When we make love, why don't you ever do anything for me?"

"What's the point? You say you can't come anyway."

"Not with you."

"Are you saying that you can with someone else?"

"I just think you could try a little harder to satisfy me."

"Like how?"

She presses her hot face against his chest. "Maybe like . . . by going down on me?"

"I can't do that," says Eli sharply.

"I do it for you."

"That's different. You like doing it."

"What makes you think so?"

"Well, don't you?"

"I do it because you want me to, not because I like it."

"Well," says Eli, "I've never done it and I'm not about to start. I think it's gross to do that to a girl."

"I am not a girl any more."

"How come suddenly you're talking about this shit?"

"I've been reading. I hear other people. It's supposed to help a woman if she can't . . . you know, the other way. It even says so in the magazines."

"I'm sure! In porno shit. Lesbo trash."

"Why do you think it's gross?"

117

"I tried it once."

"With who, Lori?"

Eli stretches. "Hah! Lori wouldn't let me do that to her even if I wanted to, which I don't. It was with some girl I picked up at a bar one time and it was totally disgusting."

"One time with a total stranger and you'll never do it again?"

"I tried it and I didn't like it. What's wrong with that? Where's my smokes?"

"Probably in your shirt. Which is where you left it, on the floor."

He gropes without looking, finds his shirt, puts it on, then pulls a pack of cigarettes from a pocket and lights one. "Dykes do it to make up for the fact they don't have dicks."

Zoey shakes her head. "You're wrong. Guys do it too."

"How would you know?"

"I just do, okay?"

"Yeah, right. Nothing to do with personal experience."

"That's right."

"Whatever you say, babe."

"How about with your fingers?"

"What about my fingers?"

"Touching me down there. Or is that also gross?"

"What the fuck is wrong with you?" Eli places an ashtray on his chest. "You used to be fine with things the way they were."

"I'm trying to work through some of our problems."

"Our only problem is that you won't admit your mistake in leaving me."

"So I'm our only problem?"

"I never said that! You're putting words into my mouth."

Zoey stands quickly, dislodging the ashtray. "Why the fuck are you in my house?" she yells. "Get out!"

Eli sweeps ashes from the spread back into the ashtray. "We never have one decent time together. Why are you never satisfied?"

"I am satisfied!" Zoey screams. "When I fuck with other people. So maybe you have a problem after all. What do you think of that, Mister Perfect?"

Eli sits up straight. "What did you just say?"

She groans. "Oh shit! I'm so sorry, I should not have said that. It just slipped out. I'm really really sorry."

"But is it true? Zoey, look at me!"

"Yes," she says.

"Not only," says Eli softly, "did you just admit that you've fucked with other guys, but you're not frigid with them like you are with me. Or is that another of your lies?"

"I don't lie," protests Zoey.

"So what if one of those other guys you fucked gave you AIDS?" he asks angrily. "What if you gave it to me and I passed it on to Lori and maybe even to our baby? I trusted you! I thought the one thing I could count on was that I wouldn't have to worry so long as we kept everything between the three of us. Your fidelity was my insurance."

"I wrote to you," says Zoey. "I practically drew you out a map. Why didn't you ever write me back? Am I supposed to hang on to you forever? There's no fucking future in it, El. I don't want to be your insurance, I want a life of my own! I am not happy. I'm just not happy." She spreads her fingers across his shoulder but he jerks away.

"What the fuck is happy?" he asks bitterly. "Is that what you expect? Well I've got news for you babe, there's no such thing as happiness!" He rises, picks up his denims from the floor. Slowly he pulls them on. "I'm leaving. I have a lot to think about."

Heart pounding, she follows him down the stairs. Now that this imagined moment has finally arrived, she isn't sure. She's just not sure that she can bear to have Eli walk out of her house for the last time. Maybe forever.

At the door he turns. "What?" he asks sharply.

"You still have my keys," she says defiantly. "If you're leaving me, I want them back." Eli dips into his pocket, digs them out and tosses. Clattering, they hit the floor. He turns his back and slams the door behind himself.

119

Slowly Zoey bends to pick them up. This is it then. She has shared her secrets with him and, instead of understanding, he has gone. She holds the keys still warm from him. He only cares about insurance. She turns on the tap for clear cold Roseville water. She runs some across her wrists, then cups her hands and drinks the way she did when she was little. After moving here when she was young she had no girlfriends, but she got to read a lot and she never had to do much housework because her mom said she would have her entire adult life to cook and clean and kids should get some breaks. Mom was cool like that, but still she was a mother and a kid can't talk to a mom like she can talk to a friend. Elijah and Jerry became her friends except that they were boys and a girl can't talk to a boy the way she can to another girl. Zoey dries her hands upon the towel lying on the counter top.

If he loved me she thinks but even as she thinks it she knows the truth. Eli can't love, it isn't in him. She wonders where he went. Maybe to her private place in the woods, maybe he has stolen that from her as well. But more likely he's gone home to Lori or out to visit Jerry. The two of them cracking open beers and staring underneath the hood of his clunky old Mercedes, that piece of shit he's been working on since high school.

Being back here now, it seems as though she never left. Her mind still holds pictures of her cozy cave-like room in Jean Paul's basement and of George, soft, warm and exciting, of the ocean and the mountains, but they're all fading fast. Perhaps she will forever be a captive here.

She opens the fridge to look for something edible. Eggs and cheddar, she could scramble them together with a lot of butter. She taught herself to make cheesy eggs when Mom was sick but still at home. "At least I had a mother," Zoey tells the eggs that she is clutching.

Japanese

The tenth time he phones, she answers. "Don't hang up!" Jean Paul says quickly. "Please! I want to call a truce. I understand your concern about the child and I apologise for not having been more consolation to you. Let me take you out for Japanese to make it up."

"Fine," says George. "I'm bored with this application and I hate arguing with you."

"Yes!" he shouts triumphantly. "And hon . . ."

"Yes?"

"No panties tonight, understood?"

Once they've been seated in a booth, the waiter leaves to get their wine while Jean Paul tears the wrapping from his chopsticks. "Remember these?" he asks seductively.

George nods and licks her lips.

"I love this tablecloth," he says as his right hand disappears beneath it.

She swallows hard.

"How is that for you?" he asks in a normal speaking voice.

"Just fine," she whispers. "A teeny bit over to the left would be absolutely perfect."

"A bite of you as apéritif," he tells her, "would be lovely."

George slides forward on her chair.

"I'd like a taste," he says. "May I?"

"If you please."

"I please. Very much."

The waiter reappears. Although the second setting is unoccupied he fills its glass before discreetly leaving. Unsteadily George lifts her goblet. Lips. Teeth. "Ah," she breathes.

charity

Stacks of clothing cover every surface of her room only now she can't decide what to do with them. She can't concentrate. Probably because of the Valium she swallowed after Eli left. Before douching and after scrubbing. But first she had locked all the doors. She used to feel so close to him. She remembers feeling safe.

It's strange to think of how a man can fill a woman up so fast she doesn't even have time to notice. There are no guides. Books don't tell the truth, nor movies either. They show how women are supposed to look and act while being fucked by men, with perfect mouths and tits and asses, and how they are supposed to come. But men don't come in movies like they do in her experience, grunt and sag and yawn and fall asleep. You don't see them while they're fucking and you never see a penis hard so how do you know what it's supposed to look like?

With Eli sex usually doesn't go on long enough for her to feel much of anything. After he comes she gets sticky and has to pee and sometimes it hurts. No one ever told her how to get wet inside, she thought it was just supposed to happen if you were in love and not frigid. But Georgie made her wet with spit and fingers and then the rest was easy. Eli never paid attention to her clit and once he tried to fuck her ass, which hurt and made her mad. He said some girls liked it. She didn't know men did that to women but it sure felt good when Georgie slid in one smooth finger. George's books say the penis is like a clitoris so now she understands why he likes it when she strokes and tugs and licks and sucks him there.

Zoey is staring through her bedroom window. The sun is shining and she is warm but it already smells like autumn. She should walk through the woods. Or she should go downtown. But everything she thinks of doing makes her miss Eli more.

Sometimes she hears her mother's voice and she will turn around or look up expecting to see her there, alive. She often thinks of questions and ideas she'd like to share with her, mother-daughter things and it's the same with Eli, except he isn't dead. She talks to him inside her head all the time. They used to talk for real. He used to write little poems and read them aloud to her, but as far as she knows, the only poem he's written since his wedding is the one he read to her in the hotel room. The one he crumpled up and tossed away.

Zoey sighs and surveys the mess around her. She doesn't have to decide this very minute, it can wait. She has a week. No one is breathing down her neck. She thought she might find an agent to try to sell the house, but she doesn't need the money to survive and even if she got full price for it, it would barely make a dent in the cost of property on the coast. She isn't even sure she wants to stay out there. But this house is part of her mother's legacy and Zoey will not squander it. She can let it sit for years. It is hers to do with exactly as she pleases.

Quickly she grabs her keys and slips on her jacket. She locks all the doors. She has heard about those nice quiet guys who go crazy and slash up their girlfriends or their families. He says his mother is insane, it might be in his genes.

People in their yards are mowing grass, clipping hedges, harvesting their vegetables. All of them are busy, even little kids. She will not think about him anymore. She will enjoy her walk through the town that she grew up in.

home again

Everyone says you can't go home again but Zoey proves them wrong. She has come home and everything is the same as it was before. Maybe it hasn't been long enough, maybe they mean years and years. But people smile through her and ask her how she's doing, nothing more and nothing less, just like always. She could slip right back and no one would notice. Lori would get bigger and eventually she'd pop that baby and Eli might decide who he wanted. Or not. Either way, in Roseville there are other married guys who'd give their teeth to have a mistress just like her.

Main Street hasn't changed. She checks her mail box at the post office out of habit and sure enough the postcards she sent to herself along the way have arrived. She shoves them in her backpack.

At the Family Fare she picks out cans of vegetable soup, crackers and imported cheese to show that she doesn't give a shit about mad cow disease. Several cartons of cigarettes and a three-pack of disposable lighters. While she waits in line to pay, she feels a tap on her shoulder and when she turns she is face-to-face with Lori.

"It *is* you! I thought you looked familiar."

"Oh hi," says Zoey.

"Long time no see," says Eli's wife. "Eli said that you were out of town."

"I was."

"Oh. So are you back to stay?"

"Only for a week."

"And then you'll be going back to . . ."

"Vancouver," says Zoey promptly before remembering that Lori isn't supposed to know. Too late. "I heard about the baby," she says quickly.

Lori pats her belly. "Yes," she says proudly. "I'm due in spring."

The cashier begins to ring up her purchases and Zoey turns to watch. Lori taps her arm. "Since when were you in Vancouver?"

"I . . . I wasn't," stammers Zoey, blushing. "Actually I've been in Calgary. I'm on my way out to the coast."

"I really love Vancouver! Eli and me went there for our honeymoon."

"I think I remember that."

"Eli was there a few weeks ago for a conference. That guy! He's so romantic! He even stayed at the same hotel because it reminded him of me."

"No kidding."

"Well I really should get going, I have to get the shopping done. I just had to see if it was really you." She walks away proudly, jutting out her abdomen as far as she can force it.

That's all it takes to make her happy, a baby in the oven and a lying stinking cheating husband she can call her own. He would not even have remembered the hotel without Zoey's prompting. This, coming from the guy who claims he can't stand bullshit.

When she opens her back door, a note flutters to the stoop and she unloads her bags on the counter before retrieving it. *Did the guys you went with wear condoms? I have a right to know. I'll be at the office till five o'clock. Phone me there.* Zoey turns the page. There should be more but she can't find it. Just *me, me, me!* She picks up the phone. "I got your note," she tells him.

"Where have you been all day? I could've left here an hour and a half ago."

"So? Why didn't you?"

"Are you going to answer my questions?"

"Like you answer mine when I write to you?"

"Touché! I bet you've been wanting to say that for awhile."

"I guess."

"Was it worth the wait?"

"You can be such a prick."

125

"I thought you didn't like to use that word."

"Why leave me a note like this? It's just plain mean. I thought you weren't like that, but I guess I was wrong. Oh by the way, I saw Lori at the grocery store."

"Did she see you?"

"Yup. And she couldn't wait to talk to me. She asked me where I've been and I said Vancouver without thinking. But then I realised she might put two and two together so I told her I've been in Calgary."

"Did she believe you?"

"I think so."

"I've been thinking . . ." He pauses.

"What?"

"About that stuff, you know." His voice is gruff. "That stuff you said you wanted me to do. When we fuck."

"Oh."

"I've never given it much thought before. Everyone else seems happy with the way I do it. Even you, till now. But I was thinking that maybe I should try it your way. Let me come over and make us dinner and whatever happens, happens."

"Okay," says Zoey. Then she hangs up quickly. That way neither of them can change their mind.

giving

He moves easily around her mother's kitchen as though it belongs to him. "I invited Jer," he says. "He's got nothing else to do."

"I thought you wanted us to be alone."

"He's my alibi. Anyway he really wants to see you and he's got reefer. Also he's going to bring a video. Pass me that knife, the smallest one."

Jerry arrives laughing and scoops her in his arms, then spins with her around the room.

"Put me down this instant!" she shrieks, kicking wildly. "Help! Eli, help!"

"He can't help you now!" teases Jerry. "I've got you and I'm never going to let you go. You can sit on my lap while I spoon-feed you."

"I don't think El would go for that." She giggles. "Would you, Eli?"

"You look good enough to eat! Doesn't she look fabulous LJ?"

"Absolutely," Eli says heartily. "But you won't have to eat *her*. Dinner's on."

After they eat Zoey starts to clear the table but Eli stops her with a smile. "We've spent the last two hours in this kitchen, babe. Let's take a break, have a toke. Jer brought a movie."

"I'll be right there," she says and when she returns from the bathroom they make room for her between them on the couch.

Jerry lights the joint he's chewing on. "You still do this, right?"

"You bet she does," Eli answers.

"You wouldn't believe this pot we smoked one time," says Zoey. "It was just insane."

"Who's we?" Jerry asks.

"Me and my boss and her boyfriend."

Eli takes the joint. "Zoey's living with her boss's boyfriend."

Jerry smirks. "Kinky!"

Eli rolls his eyes. "Put in that vid now bud."

Unsteadily Jerry rises. "Maybe I should just fast-forward to the good parts."

"Shhh," says Eli. "Hey babe, have another hoot."

"This is just a roach."

"Jer! Get with the program, man."

Jerry presses play, lights another joint and passes it to Zoey. They smoke and watch the video, then Eli tells her to stretch out and she does, lays her head upon his lap. Jerry lifts her feet and places them on his thighs while on the screen the woman stretches between two men in the exact same position. Zoey grinds her toes into his crotch like the woman in the movie. He grabs her foot and holds it to his erection. "Now you know why they call me Big Boy," he mimics. When the actor pulls her shirt over her head to release her breasts, so does Zoey. Jerry grins. "Hey, LJ! I think your plan is working."

Eli grunts, breathing hard. He slides his hand along her body and tugs her skirt up to her waist. "Take off her panties Jer," he says.

Zoey lifts her bum. Her cunt is throbbing the way it is supposed to, the way it happens when she is with George. She feels how wet she is when Jerry takes her underwear. Then he removes his jeans, kicks their clothes aside and drums his fingers on her thighs while on the television Big Boy does the same. "Ask her!" he says impatiently.

Zoey looks up at Eli. "I told him he could eat you out," he explains. "You said you wanted it and he says he likes doing it."

"It's okay with me," she says softly, "if it is with you."

"Why not?" He shrugs. "I get to watch."

"Okay, but you have to take your jeans off too."

When he undresses his prick flips against his belly. He sits again, setting her head back on his lap.

Jerry's tongue flickers on her slit. "You like that?" he asks thickly. "Does this feel nice?"

Eli's dick dribbles onto her cheek and she licks its spill. She stretches up her arms and he grasps her tits with both his hands while Jerry digs around her cunt with insistent fingers hard. Eli slides his cock between her open lips. On the screen, someone's being shot. "Oh fuck!" she gasps. "Fuck! Oh fuck, oh fuck, oh fuck."

"I guess that means she likes it," Jerry says, losing contact with her for a moment.

Zoey whimpers, arching up towards him, and Eli groans. "Fuck her, man! Shove it in. She wants you to."

She spreads her legs apart and, moving slowly, Jerry rocks his slender prick inside. He strokes into her cunt with it for awhile, then he pulls it out and teases her over onto her belly. He could do anything to her right now and she wouldn't mind a bit. She lifts her pelvis and he cups his hand around it from the back, jerking off her clit while poking deep with one smooth finger. With his other hand he slaps her bum. She is throbbing from his tugging and his probing; she is hot and tingling from his spanking.

"My turn," Eli pants.

Zoey tumbles to the floor pulling them along. Jerry bites her nipples, Eli rubs his cock along her snatch. Both their pricks are beating on and into her, Eli's fatter, Jerry's longer. In and out, first one and then the other, then both of them together. She shudders and convulses, her voice is raw and hoarse from panting. Eli pushes back to watch her come while Jerry rests against her. He laughs delightedly. "Awesome baby!"

"Water!" Zoey croaks.

Eli leaps to his feet, dashes to the kitchen and returns with a full pitcher. "Now are you satisfied?" he asks while she guzzles. "Was that enough for you?"

"I'm sore all over," she complains. "What did you guys do to me? I have to pee like crazy." She jumps up.

"Wow!" Jerry slides his hand along his dick. "That was wicked! Are you sure you want to let that pussy go?"

"Jesus you're a pig!"

"Hey man, this was your idea. I thought you told me she was frigid."

Eli shakes his head. "I've never seen anything like that before! I don't think it's normal."

"Obviously it's your decision, but I'd hang on like hell if it was up to me."

"Well it's not," Eli snaps. "What you don't seem to get is that fucking isn't everything. Here's your pants. You'd better go."

In the bathroom Zoey inspects her body. Her butt is hot, pink-streaked from Jerry's hand. It feels so good. She has been folded inside-out but there is no blood. She takes a shirt hanging from a hook and slips it on. "You guys should go," she tells them from the doorway.

"I'm outta here," says Jerry. "I'll be seeing you." He pecks her cheek as he passes, quickly waves at Eli and then dashes out.

Zoey sits quietly beside her sullen married boyfriend, still naked on the couch. "Well?" he asks after awhile.

"Well what?"

"You're cool?"

"Are you?"

"Why not? It went exactly like I planned it."

"You shit!"

"Hey! I thought you said that it was cool."

"Do you always have to be in control?"

"You liked it right?"

"Yeah, I liked it."

"Well okay then." He pulls her closer. "So why be mad? It was a gift from me to you. I planned it to make you happy."

"But it didn't make you happy, did it? You don't believe in being happy."

"But you do."

"Can you stay the night?"

"Nah . . . Lori is expecting me. We go to church on Sunday."

"Of course," she says. "Of course. You have to go. To ease your guilt if nothing else."

Sunday suit

She was wrong about church easing guilt. Elijah squirms all through the service. Like a little boy tucked into his scratchy Sunday suit, he can't sit still. Lori's eyes are stern upon him and he half-expects to hear her scold or shush him, or order him to wait out in the car.

Underneath his suit his prick is permanently stiff. Images of Zoey from last night keep flashing through his mind. He aches to hold her but he knows that this time he has fucked it up, probably for good. In one fell swoop he has discarded his two best friends.

In the pew beside him his prize wife cradles her swelling belly with possessive palms.

another trap

On Sunday morning Zoey opens her back door to find out if it's warm enough for shorts and there is grinning Jerry on her stoop. "I thought I'd stop by since I happen to know LJ's in church. Check on how you're doing, if there's anything you need, whatever. To thank you for last night. You got some coffee? Beer?"

"No beer." Zoey leads him inside. "But the coffee's on and I have wine."

He pulls out a chair and slides his stash-pouch from his pocket. "Wine with this," he says, "would be absolutely primo."

Zoey uncorks a bottle, fills two glasses and sets one in front of Jerry who trades it for the reefer he has lit.

He coughs out smoke. "Life's a bitch and then you die."

"I guess."

"Did LJ take that video?"

"I don't remember."

"Maybe he wants to watch it with the wife to see if anything interesting pops up."

"Maybe."

"In case I haven't mentioned it, I really loved last night."

Zoey pushes back her chair. "Let's go listen to some music. Grab your glass and ashtray." She inserts a tape, presses play then sits beside him on the couch, brushing away his hand insistent on her leg.

He sighs. "You know something? I don't think LJ deserves you."

"I don't think so either."

"I've never known what you see in him. He has no imagination. At work he takes care of nuts and bolts; I do the creative shit. I don't know why I'm telling you, you were there. And the way he treats you makes me crazy."

"It's my fault too," says Zoey. "I let him get away with it."

"Excuse me, but I think that's crap. Any other guy would've figured out long ago what it takes to make you happy."

"Fucking isn't everything."

"That's what he says too. But it's a damn good start."

"He's always been there when I needed him."

"Like when? Every time he got himself another babe he kicked you out."

"I thought you two agreed on everything."

Jerry rubs his shoulder blade and frowns. "Even though last night kind of turned him on, I think he was disgusted by it too. I don't think he even likes doing it. Lori probably is perfect for him. Fucking to procreate, not for fun."

"Yeah, I know."

"I really want him to get caught."

"I think I've figured out what he was up to by setting up the two of us."

"What's that?"

"He was turning me from a girlfriend into just another fuck."

After he leaves, Zoey gathers boxes and large plastic bags and hauls them upstairs. Then she sorts through all her clothing. She packs winter wear like boots and scarves and mittens into sturdy boxes and labels them. She packs thick socks, sweaters and heavy jeans as well, keeping out a few favourites because she gets so cold on the coast when it rains. Things she no longer wants she separates for give-away.

The past is just another trap. She will try to bury faulty memories. She will work at letting go. Whether the future holds George or Xandra or Corey or someone she hasn't even met yet, she won't ever have to settle. She has her independence thanks to Mother; she still has some choice.

sweet dreams

"But if they choose to do it," argues Nancy, who has taken to calling late-night from New York. "Criminalising activity doesn't make it stop, it just shoves it further underground. Which not only makes it much more lucrative, but adds the appeal of getting into something the ruling class considers both illegal and immoral."

"I never said it should be criminalised! I said we should eliminate the causes. It's exploitation to cut a profit from people's weakness."

"You see? You consider it weak to crave humiliation. You think it's a disease that should be cured. But it's neither weakness nor disease. Submission and domination are the pinnacles of love. That's why mistress-slave relationships are so intensely satisfying. And, if you acknowledge it or not, the politic of sex is power. If a consenting adult chooses to pursue something that fulfils them, no matter how twisted you think it is, they should have the right and it should be no one else's business. What would you do if it were criminal for you to fuck with women or whomever else you choose?"

"It depends. If I wanted to fuck with kids or someone who I had to force," says George. "If an abused child grows up wanting to be degraded, that's not free choice, it's conditioning. What we don't need is more freedom to damage one another."

"Not every kid who was abused grows up like me, I can assure you. If they did, we'd be the majority. But forget that, let's talk profit. If someone opens up a private club where we can go to act out our fantasies safely with other people who also choose to be there, and she profits from it, is that exploitation? All she's offering is a safe place to do what we'll do anyway. Backstreet abortionists versus clean clinics, it's exactly the same issue. Women will always need and get abortions just as those of us who are into pain will always find some way to satisfy our needs."

George flinches. "Why do you keep on saying *we*?"

"Because I feel the need to remind you that this is not some lofty academic exercise for me, it's who I am. Your problem is you won't admit it."

"But I know you! Sadomasochism is not the sum total of who you are."

"The boundaries I've constructed between who I am, what I want and how I create have gotten fairly flimsy. In fact they're nonexistent, if you want to know the truth."

George sniffs. "It sounds like you've been indulging yourself."

"So what if I have? What gives you authority to pass judgment? I crave public recognition and private degradation. Bringing those elements together in my work seems logical to me. What's your handy pocketbook psychology on that?"

"I'm not sure," says George slowly. "But I don't agree that it's your own free choice. Didn't your father punish you whenever you accomplished something? Didn't he teach you to accept pain as your reward? It's how you were conditioned, and now you find a way to do it for yourself. You feel you don't deserve anything you've earned."

"You could not be more wrong!" retorts Nancy angrily. "I *know* I deserve every ounce of recognition I can get. I have suffered endlessly for my fucking art!"

"But still, it's the pattern he established. You have to suffer to be valued."

"What the fuck! What the earthly fucking hell would you know about my asshole-fucking father?"

"All I know is that he demanded perfection and he was abusive."

"Then you don't know a blessed holy fucking thing."

"Tell me," George pleads, "what it is that I don't know."

"You'd never sleep again, that's what you don't know. *Abuse* does not begin to scratch the surface of what that prick-dog-pussy-mangler-bastard did to me. I was still a baby when he had utter and complete control."

135

"I know," says George apologetically. "You're absolutely right, I haven't got a clue. I just wish you'd tell me."

"Don't sweat it," Nancy says flippantly. "My daddy spoiled me rotten; he ruined me for anybody else. He's the only one I'll ever truly love."

"So you say."

"Face it, you can't fix me because I am not broken. I'm irredeemable."

"I can't believe that. No one is, not even you."

Nancy snorts. "You have this simplistic faith in triumph over adversity. Probably it's all that literary bullshit you've ingested, all that sappy Judeo-Christian-Disney ideology in which the white knight always triumphs in the end. Where good and bad are black and white. It's a comfy little theory, but it's a lie. It's a lie invented by the fat smug ruling class who don't give a good goddamn about equality or freedom, not yours or mine or anyone else's. All they care about is keeping us in line so they stay rich and powerful. Pseudo-morality for the masses is a method of control. And when you get right down to it, there is no such beast as free choice. From the cradle to the grave, we're all manipulated all the time."

"That's one thing we agree on," says George heavily. "Maybe this conversation has been soothing you, but it won't cure my insomnia. Eating you out would be so much better."

"The simple fact is I like pain with pleasure. Being hurt turns me on, it makes me hot, it makes me come soooo good. As you well know. There's someone at my door. I have to go."

"But it's after midnight here! Isn't it too late for company?"

"Depends upon the company you keep. Sweetest dreams, my precious!" Then she hangs up to welcome in god knows what.

George will never know for certain what Nancy's father did to her while she was his sole possession. It's enough to know what legacy he passed along. That he hanged himself is a mercy, but he should have done it sooner. He should have put an end to it before he did the damage.

on a stump

He calls Monday morning from the office, listens to Zoey's phone ring and ring. Hangs up at last and pulls out a file he's been working on but he can't concentrate. Sheri sticks her head around the doorway to say she's leaving to do the banking. "Have you seen Jer yet?" he asks.

"He came and left awhile ago."

"Did he say where he was going?"

"Nope. Sorry."

"I have to go out too," says Eli.

"Should I stay until you get back?"

"No, no. You go on. I'll wait."

Sheri flicks hair from her eyes. "Tell him there's a message on my desk."

"Anything I should know about?"

"I don't think so. Is that all?"

She leaves and Eli spins his chair around, noticing his fern needs water. When he passes by her desk for the watering can he sneaks a peek at Jerry's message. Only Mrs. Schmidt about her deck again. Thinks about his best friend's mouth on his mistress. Could not imagine Lori wanting that, but then she is a wife and soon to be the mother of his child.

He wishes he could talk to his dad, but the two of them have never really talked. *Take out the garbage, what's for supper, wash your hands,* stuff like that. His dad would think he had gone crazy if he suddenly started to discuss their common problems like mistresses and wives. Dad pretends no one knows about his other woman. Eli reaches for the phone again, punches Zoey's number without thinking, then counts to forty before hanging up.

On a stump in the woods Zoey contemplates her past and future. Last time she was here summer was still fresh. New yellow sun, rich young leaves, cool heavy soil. Now the leaves are turning and the air carries autumn's wistful tang. Here is her childhood. She won't let go of everything. Beside the stump on which she sits is her baby's final bed. There is no marker because she doesn't need one. Some memory is permanent. Later she will go to the graveyard by the church where her mother's body lies and set flowers on it. It's time to settle with the past.

a shoulder

Maybe Jerry thinks Eli's never done a thing for her but Zoey remembers differently. When her mom was sick he lent a shoulder. Sometimes the shoulder was for crying on, although not often because she's never been much for crying. But Mom was angry all the time and she took it out on whoever was the handiest and that was Zoey. The anger was for the grief of having to let go, Zoey understood but it was hard to take. Eli cooked meals and carried them in to her on a tray, then he'd stay to talk or read or listen to her so Zoey could slip out. He stuck by her the whole time, and later helped her with the burial. Wasn't that some kind of love?

She lays flowers on her mother's grave and walks heavily back home, puttering around the yard awhile before going in to open up a tin of soup. Easily she chews and swallows food that she is friendly with, then takes her bowl with her to see who's at the door.

"Hi again," says Lori brightly. "Can I come in?"

"Uh," says Zoey. "Actually I'm busy."

Lori pushes out her belly. "I was passing by and I thought I'd stop in to see you. We had such a short chat the other day. But if it's inconvenient . . ."

"It is," says Zoey, "inconvenient." She sets her bowl down on the stoop. "Unless there's something that you need."

Lori is flushed. "I was just hoping we could talk a bit while you're in town. You and Eli have always been so close it's almost like the two of us are sisters."

"I'm expecting someone."

"Maybe I could call? Maybe we could get together once before you leave. Have coffee."

"I'm only here till Sunday and there's still an awful lot for me to do."

"I'll phone."

Lori sails back down the path and Zoey bites her tongue on calling after her. The only thing they have in common is Eli so what is there for them to talk about? She bends down for her bowl and when she stands she bumps right into Jerry.

"Did I just pass Lori?"

"Look at me!" says Zoey. "I'm shaking like a leaf!"

He slings an arm around her. "Let's go inside."

In the living room she sprawls into a chair. "She says she thinks of us as sisters. Because Eli and me are 'close'."

"How did you get rid of her?"

"I told her I was expecting company."

"She probably thought you meant LJ."

"I don't want her precious husband."

"You should tell her so. Ease her mind."

"Let him do the easing. I didn't marry her."

"I think you should tell her all about her cheating husband."

Zoey frowns. "Do you think she's prettier than me?"

"You're way prettier," says Jerry loyally.

"I am not. I'm much too fat."

"You are definitely not fat."

"Am too."

"I've seen you naked and I say you aren't fat."

"Why did he choose her then?"

"Because he is an idiot. He thinks she makes life tidy." Jerry kneels on the floor beside her and slips his hand beneath the waistband of her shorts. "I think you're beautiful."

"This is not supposed to happen." Her voice is hoarse. "It just confuses everything."

Neither of them hears the back door open. "I thought I'd find you here!" Eli yells.

Zoey jumps, but Jerry just looks up at him and laughs. "Hey LJ! What are you doing here? I didn't hear you knock."

"I don't remember saying you could help yourself," says Eli tersely.

"I don't need permission," retorts Jerry. "She isn't yours to give."

"Zoey?" Eli asks but Zoey gazes at the wall behind him, not answering.

"You should keep that wife of yours on a shorter leash," Jerry says. "She dropped by here to try to talk to Zoey."

"About what?"

Zoey shrugs. "Why don't you ask her?"

Eli takes another step into the room. "What did you say to her?" he demands, raising a fist.

"Hey!" shouts Jerry, standing quickly. "Back off, man!"

"Find out for yourself," says Zoey angrily. "It's you two who should be talking. It has nothing to do with me. She's *your* wife."

"It isn't up to Zoey to protect you," Jerry adds. "And I think Lori should know the truth about her so-called marriage."

Eli's fist hits the wall. Then he turns on his heel and stomps away, slamming the door behind himself.

The anger is at having to let go. The shoulder was for resting on. She could rely on him back then.

orders

Zoey picks up on the first ring. "Hello," she says, but no one answers. "Hello," she says again. "Hello!" On the couch Jerry snores. When she hears the dial tone, she sets the receiver in its cradle. She pulls milk from the fridge. The phone rings. "Hello," she says impatiently. "Who is this?"

"It's me, Lori. I want to talk to Eli."

"He isn't here."

Lori's voice is hard. "Don't lie to me!"

"Why would I? You can't talk to him because he isn't here. Believe it or not, that's the truth."

"I know what's going on."

"What on earth are you talking about?"

"Oh jeez!" shouts Lori. "You can quit pretending! I know what's going on between you two! It has to stop! I'm ordering you to keep your hands off my husband!"

"First of all," says Zoey, "you have no right to give me orders. And second, I don't know what you mean. If you have problems with your husband it has nothing to do with me. You should talk to him."

"I've known about you all along, but I thought I'd let it run its course. After all, I'm the one he married, even though he could've had you in a second. Sooner or later he was bound to get bored with you. But things are different now. We're starting a family and I won't have you wrecking it. So, if you know what's good for you, you'll get out of town once and for all. And don't try to make this into some kind of war because you know I'll win. I'm his wife. We have a good marriage."

Zoey rubs her sweaty palms along her jeans. "It doesn't sound like such a good marriage to me. You don't even trust him."

"I'm warning you," says Lori coldly. "I'm the mother of his unborn child."

Zoey swallows hard. "I know you're pregnant, Lori," she says softly. "I know that. Please believe me, I would never do anything to hurt your baby."

"Well," says Lori. "I only have your word on that, but it will have to do. I guess that's all I have to say."

Gently Zoey sets down the receiver. She opens the refrigerator. She pulls out everything she can find to stuff into her mouth. She chews and swallows, chews and swallows till she can't feel anything at all.

waiting

"I'm leaving town for a few days," Jean Paul says. "Would you mind checking on the house from time to time?"

"Sure," says George. "No problem. Have you heard from Zoey yet?"

"No. Haven't you?"

"Not a word."

"I'm sure she'll be okay."

"It's just that I need her back. For work."

"Why would you think she won't come back?"

"If she's gone home . . ."

"She could be doing the tourist thing. Maybe she's in Seattle."

"I doubt it. Where are you going?"

"Edmonton. I'd ask you to come . . ."

"No thanks," says George. "Waiting here is bad enough."

"Did you say waiting? What are you waiting for?"

"Everything. Zoey, Nancy . . ."

"Why in the world would you wait for Nancy?"

"I'm not!" George says quickly. "What I am is worried sick about this application."

"Give yourself a break. You're an accomplished writer; you deserve a grant."

"Unfortunately that doesn't seem to have much to do with it," she says dryly. "What time is your flight?"

"Insanely early. When did you say Nancy is coming back?"

"I didn't. I haven't got a clue. She's getting sleazy in the rotten apple. She's taken an apartment."

"Sleazier than usual?"

"Should I water the plants and check your messages? Or should I just walk by?"

"Don't go to any trouble. I'll be home by Saturday."

George hangs up the phone and leans back in her chair. Sunlight sprays her shoulders, reminding her of Zoey's constant complaints about rain. Now she's missed the best part of August. If she has returned to the Prairies, chances are she won't return. And Nancy's new apartment might be permanent. Which leaves Jean Paul. George shudders and gets back to her application.

filling up

The first time he caught her puking Eli froze her out for a month. It was his dinner she was getting rid of and he took it as an insult. But the closer death came to her mother, the more he cooked, the more she puked. She couldn't help it. All his girlfriends did it, all of them behind his back were filling up the toilets with his food so that they could stay as thin and perfect as he expected them to be.

clues

George lets herself into Jean Paul's house, depositing her sandals on the mat because he is fussy about shoes worn inside. The place is immaculate as always. He claims he can't create when his life is out of order.

She takes water from the fridge with her down the stairs to search for clues. Two slips of paper on the bedside table, Corey's number and that woman Xandra's business card. She replaces them precisely. The painting Zoey said reminded her of hell is hung again. She probably put it up before she left in case he noticed. George opens the bedside drawer, but except for a single unframed photograph, it's empty. A petite unsmiling red-haired woman wearing a good pink suit and thick glasses. The nose, forehead and eyebrows match but where Zoey's mouth is generous with smiles, the mother's lips are taut. It doesn't look as though she had much fun, a single mom in small-town Manitoba working for the government. George turns the photo over. *Phyllis McTavish. Age 39, April 17, 1988.* There are no other photographs in the room, no images of other friends or family, Zoey must have left those things back home. No diary in a scribbler, no notebooks or letters. One packaged toothbrush in the bathroom, a full bottle of shampoo and three of Jean Paul's beautifully monogrammed towels.

George leaves the basement room. Jean Paul's office houses business correspondence neatly filed, a blank pad by the phone, his cardex of rich and famous others. If he were a writer there would be littered hints. Writers spread their thoughts all over and then they publish them for all the world to read. Writers leave a paper trail.

George doesn't know what she is searching for although she is most surely curious about that marriage contract he says he has been drafting. Maybe he is creating it in his mind. But if it doesn't exist on paper it's intention only and therefore doesn't mean a goddamn thing.

She replaces the water bottle in the fridge, slides into her sandals and locks the door carefully behind herself. Back at home, she picks up her cordless and on a whim she dials directory assistance in Manitoba. "Roseville," she says. And then, "McTavish." Rapidly she presses the eleven digits. "Hi!" she shouts. "Zoey? Is that you?"

"Yeah it's me. Why are you yelling? George?"

"I'm sorry, I'm just so relieved to hear your voice. I didn't expect to find you there."

"Oh. Well, you did. How are you?"

"Fine. I'm fine. How are you?"

"Alive."

"That's promising."

"I'm glad you think so."

"What's wrong?"

"Just the same old shit hitting the same old fan. Nothing's changed out here. You know small towns."

"Actually I don't. When are you leaving?"

"I'm coming back on Sunday."

"Are you flying?"

"Yup."

"I could pick you up. Tell me when you're coming in."

"Hold on a sec, I have to check my ticket . . . Arrival is two-fifteen Vancouver time."

"I'll meet you," George says. "I'll be at the luggage carousel, okay?"

"Sure."

"I miss you."

"I guess I'll see you Sunday."

Jerry sits up, yawning. "Who were you just talking to?" he asks, rubbing his eyes.

"Just my boss George. She called me from Vancouver."

"Why?"

"I think she's worried that me and Eli might get back together and that I won't be leaving after all."

"Did you know Eli thinks you got it on with her?"

"Did he tell you that?"

"Yeah, after seeing you in Vancouver. He thinks it is disgusting."

"He's an asshole."

"Was he right?"

"I'll never tell."

Jerry shrugs. "It's up to you," he says. "It's not my business. But you should know I don't agree with him. I don't have a problem with it. Not at all. Whatever turns you on is fine by me. I think women with women or guys with guys is totally okay."

"You know what?" Zoey asks. "So do I. I didn't used to, but then I didn't ever think about it much."

Jerry rises. "I should be going now. It's getting late."

"I wish you'd stay the night."

"Are you sure?"

"I'm sort of scared to be alone here after all the shit that's happened."

"Okay." He laughs. "I'll be your bodyguard if you tell me what it's like when women fuck."

Zoey picks up a cushion, tosses it between her hands, then fires it at him. "In your dreams," she chuckles.

poised

Sometimes you attach yourself to someone for absolutely no good reason but you're stuck and no amount of hell or distance can unstick you. At five-thirty in the morning, Zoey wakes straight up. Wakes up suddenly with tight throat and pounding heart. The panic dream she always has that ends up with her mother vanishing and Eli taking someone else's hand. The exact same dream. She stumbles up from bed to smoke a joint and when she crawls back in she is shivering.

"Why are you so cold?" Jerry asks, sliding close behind her.

"Just a dream," she mumbles. "Go to sleep. It's nothing."

"It must be something if it woke you up. You want to talk?"

"About my dream?"

"Sure."

"I suppose it's more a series of images than it is a dream."

"Is it scary or does it make you sad?"

"Both, I guess."

"Do you have it often?"

"Yeah. About a million times."

"I have dreams like that."

"Oh," says Zoey. "Do they make you feel like you're no good and there's totally no use to anything in your life at all?"

"Yeah."

"I guess it means I'm scared of being left."

His lashes brush her cheek. "You never have to be alone again if you don't want to be," he whispers.

She shudders. "Is that some kind of promise?"

"You can take it to the bank."

"What does it mean?"

"I think it means I love you," he says solemnly. "It means I'll be there for you for as long as you want."

In the morning she awakens on a sun-drenched pillow. He's left a note propped against a vase which holds a single red geranium that he must have gotten from the yard. Geraniums were her mother's favourite because of how they bloom all summer, into autumn and all winter too if you do it right. She smiles. *I hope you got some sleep after all. I don't want to wake you but I have to go to work. See you later. Love Jerry.*

Naturally the phone is ringing. It could be Jerry. It could be George. But it might be Eli. Or it might be Lori. She leaps up and dashes down the stairs. Then she stands glaring at the shrieking phone with her hand poised above it.

Sometimes someone gets ahold of you inside and there is absolutely nothing you can do about it. She might be able to pry Eli from her heart. She has wrenched herself away from him more times than she can count already, every time he found himself another lover and then again when he met Lori who won over them all. She has left this place, her home too for what that's worth, and has found herself another place on earth where someone says she cares enough to miss her. This tearing at herself has been never-ending; she should be used to it by now. She should be good at it by now. But every time she loses one more layer of herself. Soon there will be nothing left of her at all.

Here she is in her very own home where she has done no wrong and should be safe. She should be able to answer her own telephone without being shaken up with shame or fear. Angrily she picks up the receiver. "Hello," she barks.

"Oh good, you're up." It's Jerry.

"Yeah, just barely. Is Eli at the office yet?"

"Nope. He's late."

"Lori called last night while you were asleep. She told me she knows about us and ordered me to stay away from him. Get out of town, she said. Maybe that's why he's late."

151

"How did she find out?"

"How would I know? Maybe it's those stupid pictures he always takes of me. Or she could've found a letter." Through the window above the sink she watches sparrows pecking seed from the feeder. "What if he goes nuts and tries to do something to me?"

"I'll be right over," he says. "Sit tight."

As soon as she hangs up the phone it starts to ring again. It's still ringing when Jerry knocks. She lets him in and points to it. "I know it's him," she says. "He just won't quit."

"Let me answer it. If it is, I'll tell him to stop harassing you."

"Okay."

She wraps her arms around him from behind and he picks up the receiver. "Hello," he says briskly. "Listen buddy, she doesn't have to talk to you and she doesn't have to take your crap. Don't fuck with me! So? You can't blame her! Who left them around for her to find? What's your problem? No, I said what's yours?"

Zoey feels his voice vibrating through his sweater. "What's he saying?" she whispers.

Jerry holds one finger up. "Take a pill, have a shower, see a preacher, whatever. I'll be here all day so don't even think of doing something stupid. You'll have to go through me." He slams down the receiver. "Let me make some coffee," he says. "I need to do something useful with my hands. Jesus! What a jerk!"

Zoey opens the cupboard and passes filters and the coffee tin then watches while he measures, scoops and pours. "He and Lori had a fight and she's gone home to mommy, am I right?"

He turns on the coffee maker. "How did you know?"

"She's the type."

"It sounds as if he blamed it all on you. I think he claimed you lured him and he couldn't help himself. He thinks you told her but you didn't, did you?"

"Of course not!" Zoey is indignant. "I didn't tell her anything. I tried to cover up for him."

"I know, I know. You heard what I said to him." The coffee maker sputters. "I hope it's not too strong for you. I like it strong." She opens the refrigerator. "Me too. You take milk?"

Sometimes you attach yourself to someone for no good reason and then there's not a goddamn thing you can do about it. No amount of being hurt or common sense can unglue you. Sometimes a heart just stops beating without apparent rhyme or reason. And what the fuck is in a dream?

Warhol minutes

Nancy has dropped all pretense of impartiality. No longer the observer, thoroughly she weaves herself into the fabric of experience which she recreates on canvas. When David Bowie proclaimed death as performance art, the only thing he did was to report reality. One thing is certain; bodies are a dime a dozen. There are thousands in the world, some just for the taking and others for a price, most of whom would not be missed if they disappeared. Some speculate that serial killers or even aliens are responsible for the missing persons and surely some of those do exist because every so often they locate credible abductees or expose a Paul Bernardo. Or a Dahmer holding cut-up corpses in his cupboards. But bodies can be chewed and swallowed up.

Like every successful commercial artist, Nancy Rider knows her market. She understands the appetite of the public is insatiable, it gobbles up macabre fuck-and-torture dished out by supermarket tabloids and Hollywood and there are no borders in the game of consuming humans, it is an international obsession. From Miss Baby Teens to rats thrust up vaginas, from cigarette-scabbed vulvas to naked infants advertising milk or soap or cameras, from priests molesting children in their care to clitoridectomies, from burning brides to nine-year-olds on stage shoving blades into their cunts for cheering businessmen. In fact, as Nancy sees it, there is scant difference between what her father did to her when she was his charge and what she does to earn a living now. Distinction is a matter of perspective. All markets are determined by consumption, product to meet demand.

Bodies are a dime a dozen. It's a greedy loveless world and most people in it will do anything to get their Warhol minutes in the spotlight or just for cold hard cash. Developing nations have realised that there is a global market for their massive crops of undernourished children. They can be harvested for organs, they can be bartered out as sex-slaves to the wealthy who crave the ultimate erotica of their utter lack of power. Much more lucrative than trying to scratch crops out of dead and dying dirt. It's simple economics: ethics are for the middle classes; the very rich have no use for them and the very poor cannot afford them.

There is a global market for Nancy's talent. The Frankfurt people have agreed to handsome recompense to protect her against potential loss of status, but having dipped her feet into that pool and found it welcoming, she knows there won't be any. The mainstream has been desensitised and the fact that the middle class has all but disappeared world-wide can't hurt either. Frankfurt is her ticket to the international stature she has striven for and deserves, and it will prove her worth to those few pedestrian critics who still refuse to recognise the new world order which has expanded far beyond their obsolete morality.

VOWS

After some negotiation, the three of them have agreed to meet. Jerry and Zoey walk over together and Eli greets them at the door, then he leads them to his office where he takes the chair behind his desk. Zoey sits across from him in the steno chair and Jerry perches on a corner of the desk between them.

Eli clears his throat. "This is awkward for all of us, I guess," he says. "I don't really know how to start."

"You're the one who called this meeting," says Zoey. "So you should have the floor."

Eli studies his shoes intently. "If you think that this is easy . . ." He takes a deep breath. "Alright then, I guess I'll start. I want to know why you have betrayed me."

Jerry spins to face him. "Who precisely is your accusation aimed at? And what exactly do you mean by 'betrayed'?"

Carefully Eli folds the fingers of two hands inside each other. He fiddles with his wedding band. "*Who* precisely is the both of you. And *what* exactly is telling Lori."

"What makes you think either of us told her?" asks Jerry calmly.

"How else would she find out?"

"You should talk about betrayal," Zoey says wearily. "What I still can't figure is why you'd marry someone you think is too damn stupid to guess about her cheating husband. Especially when he leaves so many clues around it might seem like he wants her to find out."

"If you didn't tell her, who did?"

Zoey snorts. "Oh come on El! Even you can't be this dumb. Maybe she found some of my letters or those naked pictures you keep on taking.

She could've known about us all along like she claimed. Maybe she's been pretending not to know because it was easier for her that way."

"Or maybe," Eli interrupts, "if she hadn't seen you at the store the other day, she wouldn't have gotten suspicious in the first place."

"How long am I supposed to stay in hiding for your protection?"

"Any way you look at it," Jerry says, "you can't blame Zoey. It's your own damn fault; you've broken your vows and now you have to pay for it."

"I'll bet *you* told her! You're jealous of me! You couldn't face the fact that Zoey always liked me better, and you couldn't deal with my getting married either. I have all the things you've always wanted. You've never even had one decent girlfriend."

"I think she's known about us all along," Zoey interjects.

"You stay out of this!" Eli shouts. "This is between me and Jer. I hope you're satisfied! By ratting out on me, not only do you end up with the girl, but you also get to fuck up my marriage while you're at it. Plus you get to be the hero."

Jerry grins. "You're right about a few things, buddy," he says. "I have been jealous of you and Zoey. I never thought that you were worthy of her. You've treated her like shit ever since we were kids. You acted like she was a piece of trash you could pick up and discard at whim. But it wasn't me who ratted on you. I should have, but I didn't. It's your own fault that this is happening to you. And, just for the record, it was you who gave me Zoey. As though she were yours to give!"

The clock ticks. Eli drums upon his desk. "I can see I've made some big mistakes," he says at last. "But carrying on with her has been my biggest. I should've dumped her back in high school. I should've let you have her then."

Jerry looks suddenly at the ceiling and whistles.

Zoey gathers up her hair and knots it tightly at her neck. "Mistake," she says, her face stone-white.

"Yes," says Eli angrily. "I'm sorry, but that's the way I feel right now."

She shakes her head from side to side. "Oh god," she says. "My god! I have been so fucking stupid! All this time I've let myself believe in you!"

"I never lied to you!" he shouts. "Not about anything."

"You've never told me that you love me, that's the truth. Which you think lets you off the hook! *Some guys just can't say it,* remember that? *I'm here with you; that should be enough.* No, you never lied to me about your nonexistent feelings. But my god I am so fucking stupid!"

Eli slips his diamond-studded golden band until it catches on his knuckle. He slides it down again. "It's over," he says. "Now I have no choice."

"Eleven years," says Zoey dully. "After everything we've been through. *I've* been through. And all of a sudden I'm not worth the grief."

"Over," Eli says tersely. "That means no phone calls, no letters, no contact whatsoever."

"*Over* means an end to those morning calls checking up on me at the theatre? *Over* means no more fake conferences? No more honeymoon suites to remind you of your wife?"

"This isn't love, it's an addiction. Years and years of habit. We'll both be better off; you'll see."

Zoey lights a cigarette with shaking hands. "I've tried," she says. "I've left my home so you could hold onto yours. I moved away! Don't you see? I've been trying!"

Idly Jerry flicks his lighter. "I guess this is as good a time as any," he says, "to discuss the business. To tell you I want out."

"Jesus Jer!" explodes Eli. "What kind of friend are you? My fucking life is lying here in shambles and all you can think of is causing more destruction?"

Jerry shrugs. "We have to deal with it."

"Have I been dismissed?" asks Zoey coldly. "Should I do my nails or something?"

"Okay," says Eli. "I kind of guessed this might be coming. I'll buy you out if that's what you want. I'll get the lawyers on it."

"Right away," Jerry says.

"Don't push me Jer!" Eli snaps. "I said I'd get it done!"

"What I think," says Zoey quietly. "What I think is that you wanted to get caught. I think you left clues for Lori the same way you arranged for me and Jer to fuck. I think you did it so you wouldn't have to make your own decisions. You planned it so the rest of us would make your choices for you and you would not be responsible. I think you're a fucking coward."

"Damn it, Zoey!" Eli wrings his hands. "You've known me forever! Ever since we were eight years old! And even you can't see?"

"What should I be seeing?"

"That I'm the one who can't let go of you. It's ruining my fucking life."

"Fuck you, Eli! Don't you dare! Don't you fucking dare! I absolutely refuse to feel sorry for you now!" Zoey sets her shaking elbows on the desk beside Jerry's knees and plants her cheeks inside her palms. "You say it," she commands. "You look me in the eyes right now and spit it out. I only want to hear it once; I won't ever ask again. But I can't bear to think that this was all for nothing."

"Okay!" Eli leans across his desk. "You win! What you've always wanted. I love you! I've always loved you!" Breathing heavily, he sits back. "There, I've said it! Are you happy now?"

Zoey blinks. "Don't you get it?" she asks icily. She stands. "They're only words. That's all they are. They have no power of their own. And your saying them now doesn't change a single fucking thing."

Jerry jumps from his perch. "I'll finish up that deck job if you want. I don't intend to leave you hanging." He stretches out his hands to Zoey. "Come on. Let's go."

Left alone, Eli slouches in his chair. He gazes through his floor-to-ceiling window into darkness. Soon it will be winter and when that's done he will be a father. His wife's rounding belly sickens him. She wants three kids. Every day he thinks about a vasectomy. On the note pad beside his phone he scribbles himself a quick reminder to call his doctor.

bliss

"Twins," gushes Saffron. "Très sweet, a brother and a sister. You'll adore them. Innocent and very very blonde."

"I said how much?" Nancy asks impatiently.

Saffron rolls her eyes and sighs. "Has anyone ever told you you're no fun? No fun at all, when you're working."

"I said how much? And when can you deliver?"

"Look!" Saffron urges, trying to press a wad of photos into unresponsive hands. At last she gives up, fanning them across the bar instead. She jabs with hooked enameled nails. "The boy is submissive and the girl is dominant. They work so well together, they could be twins. Jesus, lighten up! This is about your pure and unadulterated bliss."

Nancy picks up the pictures and shuffles them between two hands like a deck of playing cards. Then she gestures at the cage hanging from the rafters. "That one too," she orders briskly. "I think I can work her in. And don't bother me about the cost."

scabs

Zoey lies across Jerry with his prick hard and still inside. Gently she rotates her pelvis, rubbing her clit against his shaft. She imagines Eli seated on this bed right now, watching. Wanting. Waves of lust wash through her. "Remember?" she whispers. "How you smacked me the other night? Remember that? With Eli, when me and you were fucking?"

"How could I forget?"

"I wish you'd do that to me again."

"Are you saying that you want a spanking?"

"Yeah. But hit me harder. Really hard. I mean hard enough to make me bleed."

"Why would you want that?"

She shrugs. "I don't know," she says shyly. "What's the difference why? I just want you to."

Jerry turns his head away. "I wish you hadn't asked."

Zoey swallows. "What's the matter with my asking?"

"I just wish you hadn't. It makes me wonder what you expect from me."

"I just told you what I want."

"Well, I don't think that I can do it."

"Why not?"

"The other night we did something that was good for both of us, right?"

"I think so."

"This is different. This is something that might be good for you, but it wouldn't be so good for me."

"Why not?"

"Because I don't think giving someone pain is all that sexy. It would turn me off. Completely."

"Oh."

"If it's to prove how bad you are, I don't want to help you do it. The way I see it, you've done nothing wrong. You don't deserve to be punished."

Inside her body, Zoey feels him withering. She clenches tight to keep him in but it's no use. He slips out and she rolls off. Her face is hot and she is grateful for the darkness. "I did not expect a lecture," she says stiffly. "I only asked."

"I'm sorry." Jerry yawns. "I want you to fuck with me because you like me. But if you want to be hurt, you'll have to get it from someone else." He curls up, away from her.

She sits. She stretches for the blankets. Slowly she pulls them up around him. She strokes his hair for just a minute, then lies still beside him. Silently she gropes around her heart. She's picking at the scabs she's used to feeling there, the endless ache that feeds her nightmares. Those bruises representing everyone she might have had and lost: Mother, Eli, baby, father, grandparents, aunts and uncles, cousins, friends. Maybe even George, who showed her passion for a passing second.

She touches Jerry's skin so hot it should be glowing and wills herself not to wish for anything. She doesn't love him in the same way she loves Eli or even George, but it would be interesting not to be abandoned, not to be deserted, not to be left for something better. Maybe she could learn to trust. Drawing heat from his body through her hand, Zoey falls asleep.

canary

It may be true that many people in this world are anonymous but when Nancy disappears she leaves a space. George hears it on the radio. *Nancy Rider . . . renowned artist . . . this morning in New York . . . Vancouver-based . . . daughter of . . . Police are searching . . .*

First she calls the CBC to confirm the story, Nancy's number next and then the cops. Dazed and in a dream, she takes the red-eye to New York and when she arrives there is a body to identify. There is no one besides George who belongs to her so she will be the one to clean the flat containing personal effects and the art she has been working on.

George has always expected people she knows will linger for awhile. When she has thought of losing friends she has imagined there would be some warning, some given time for remember-whens. A little time of grace at least, a little dignity. But there is no grace in hearing murder on the radio, no dignity in viewing someone you have madly loved lying in the morgue on a slab with her neck sliced open. Of finding yourself staring down and wondering, when it happened was she wearing that crazy fuck-me-harder grin of hers? The one that has been frozen into George's brain? The one that's ruined night upon night of sleep? The one that wakes her with a deep cold sweat every bloody time? The one she cannot, will not live without? And what oh what will she ever do without her?

Nancy's work has left with Nino when George returns at dusk. Although she is relieved to have seen the last of him and the paintings, she wishes she had taken more time alone with them. She should have waited to reach the stage beyond revulsion. Nancy's awesome vision which transformed the vulgar into the stunning and George's wicked rage at her senseless death are bound together tightly in her belly.

Nancy must have known this would happen, she must have had some premonition. She was playing in the same arena as her subjects, she should have been prepared. But if she planned for death, why now? Before Germany could give her the international recognition she craved so very badly? Frankfurt symbolised everything she had ever worked toward. And how could she have left like this, without even bothering to say good-bye?

George recalls Nancy's opinion on the providence of artists who increase the value of their work through suicide. Even in the unlikely event they find someone to identify as killer, George will never know for certain if she plotted it. Another mystery to add to those already haunting her.

Nancy was a painter not a writer, she will have left no clues except for those in her work. Or perhaps an unheeded hint in conversation loosely dropped while she obsessed about the need to cause and suffer pain. She may have wanted degradation, may have believed it was her right, but never did she express a wish to die like this. Had George asked for her opinion though, she surely would have laughed derisively. She would have proclaimed violent death as the ultimate erotic and creative act. She might have said she wanted to go out that way. Most likely she would have explained how she would enjoy it, blow-by-blow, every second, too bad it had to end. But she said such things to shock. Using George as her canary in the mine shaft, a measurement to gauge mainstream intolerance. By herself, Nancy lacked a common definition of morality.

George leans down to pick up a strappy garter belt first kicked upon the floor, then hidden underneath the bed. Tenderly, between two fingers, she lifts it to her lips to taste metallic blood. "She had her menses at the time of death," the coroner had said. "There's evidence of anal and vaginal penetration both before and after . . ." And then he had paused and waited for George to understand. He hadn't long to wait, she deals with words as a profession and she knows her Nancy. It was on the tip of her tongue but mercifully she didn't speak it, *so you went out with a bang my dear.*

When last she wore this garment, she had her period. One night long ago she had tried to patiently explain how she was weaned on father's blood instead of mother's milk, but George had kissed her into silence. Too late she wishes she had opened up her mind. Maybe Nancy could have cleared it out and then she might be alive today.

She is being selfish, luxuriating in her grief. Unsteadily she stands. Finds the telephone and, still clutching the garter belt, picks up the receiver. She presses it against her lips while dialling. Bad news travels at the speed of light so Jean Paul will have heard already. She leaves a simple message asking him to please call, reciting Nancy's New York number from her memory. Realising that she will never in her life need to call it up again.

safe

Lori has returned home to Eli who is contritely swearing to be forever faithful. What he doesn't tell her is that he's spoken to Dr. Schott about vasectomy. After all it is his body and what she doesn't know can't hurt her. He has also been to see his mother and has helped with plans to move her to a psychiatric ward in Winnipeg for electroshock to snap her from the slump she's in. He tells his wife he's through with Zoey and promises not to ever lie to her again. Unlike Zoey who is always stony-eyed, Lori weeps. He doesn't tell her that he loves her but she does not demand it. She wants simpler things from him than passion.

Neither does he mention the ring of fire in his chest causing him to ask the doctor about the condition of his heart. Schott assured him it's due to stress, nothing more. He is much too young to worry about such things and besides there is no heart disease in his family. Eli should watch his diet, stay fit, stop chasing skirts and conserve his strength for fatherhood.

He is determined to turn over a new leaf, to rid himself of the past and focus on the future. Although knowing his best friend and former mistress are spending their days and nights together won't make life less stressful, his lawyer has prepared documents for buy-out which is, to Eli's way of thinking, an unexpected bonus, something he has been considering for awhile but hasn't had the guts to bring up with Jerry. Now it's taken care of and he is not to blame.

What happens next is anybody's guess but Elijah is determined to see the silver lining. Most importantly, his marriage is intact. The business will belong to him, his mother will get well and after his vasectomy he won't be siring more unwanted babies no matter what path he chooses to travel on, even if it includes, for example, the minister's daughter who has lately often caught his roving eye in church. After the baby arrives Lori will be too involved with it to pay him much attention, and with Zoey permanently gone, she will relax.

dead babies

She sleeps to scrub away the bruises on her heart. Dreaming about the spewed-out baby pushed out and lying in-between her thighs on tall wild grass scrunched flat and wet beneath her. What she laboured for, its puckered face, squinted eyes, wrinkled ears and tiny nostrils. With her teeth she cut the cord. Then she set the body on her sunken belly, checking each digit and each orifice, skimming down the smooth slick hair as black as prairie dirt with her index finger. A girl. Born not breathing. Born dead. Who would have thought such a thing was possible?

When the sun beyond the woods began to set she scraped a shallow grave into the forest floor with her bare strong hands. She finished digging and lifted the nearly weightless body into the cradle she had made. Up above the moon rose round and white. All night she sat unthinking upon the forest floor underneath its light beside the body she had both created and destroyed. When dawn scratched the sky at last, she covered up the grave. Without a tear to shed.

Later, with warm wind flinging her skirt about, she led Eli to their baby's bed. After showing it to him she laughed and laughed. "That's some God you have!" she told him scornfully. "First He took my mother and now this. If this is His idea of justice, I don't need it."

Weeping Eli wrapped his arms around her. The silent tears spitting from his eyes sank into her hair. "Maybe you lack faith in God," he said. "I wouldn't blame you. But you know that you can always trust in me."

Zoey looked at him. Crying, but still alive and sure as always. "I have to go away," she said. "I have to leave."

"Good idea. Take some time. Think it over. Because as bad as this seems now, I think you'll see it's for the best. It never could have worked.

So go away if you have to, for awhile. Someday I think you'll realise we're better off this way."

She shook her head, staring up at leaves shivering above. "I can't make you any promises," she said.

"Are you trying to tell me you won't be coming back?"

Zoey smiled with just her mouth. "I don't know. But what I do know is that I should not have gone through this alone. There is no excuse for that."

"Wait a minute! You can't hold that against me," he protested. "You just disappeared. How was I supposed to know what was going on? You have to come back! I need you!"

"You already have everything you need," said Zoey wearily.

Eli delivered her to the bus depot in Winnipeg, leaving enough time to park his 911 on River Road and whisper hoarse endearments to her. He had a gift for her too: *50 poems* by e.e. cummings. "I'll see you soon," he said. "I'll wait for you."

She rubbed her burning eyes. "What did you say?"

"I'll be waiting for you," he repeated. "Call and let me know when you're coming back. Write to me, even if it's just a postcard. Send it to the office."

"I love you," she said quickly even though it was forbidden and then scurried past the driver into the bus. She took a seat in back. She saw him outside on the platform, scanning all the windows. When he found her he blew a kiss. Squinting she waved back, squeezing away the pictures of her baby dead upon the dirt. In the baby she saw Eli. He was right to worry, everybody would have guessed. It was much more convenient for him like this, with the two of them out of the way.

169

choices

On her mother's tombstone someone has carved an arrow-studded valentine containing two sets of initials. It doesn't bother Zoey but her mother hated vandalism. She had expected every citizen to obey the law the way she did. What she would have thought about Zoey's flouting rules these past few years is no mystery. Mother was not a follow-your-heart sort of person, she listened to her head. Life with her was an even path.

In books, characters visit graves to confide their secrets to the dead. Hidden wishes, desires and regrets. But how could she tell her mother about Eli, George or Jerry? How could she explain what she is seeking? Would Mother offer her advice she might actually apply? No. She would say, *Put your shoulder to the grindstone and do your work the best way that you can.* For her it had been that simple, she had a child to feed and clothe and house, a job to keep. Zoey has no child. She has an unimportant job. Nothing that would fall apart if she left it. Shoulder to the grindstone. Keep it simple, obey the rules and it will all work out. But it hadn't, had it? Mother died too young. Didn't she wonder then, when she was dying, what she had missed? What she could have had if she hadn't followed all the rules? If she did, she never talked about it. She was angry about the pain, not at the futility of her unlived life.

"Mom," says Zoey, feeling foolish. Then she waits. Of course there is no answer, why would there be? The earth doesn't open up, lightning does not strike nor thunder crash, the sun shines no more nor less brightly. She clears her throat. "I still love him," she tells the grass. "Even though I know it's useless. I've been such an idiot! Giving my whole life to someone who can't love." She pauses to draw a ragged breath. She hasn't cried since her mother died and she never cried for Eli once.

But you're so young.

Zoey looks around but there is not another soul in the cemetery. "If you mean to say I still have my life ahead of me," she says, "you're right. But how can I erase him? And how come it hurts so much?" She waits expectantly this time even though she knows it's silly.

You have to work at letting go.

"You never could," says Zoey, knowing suddenly. "You waited your whole life, but he never came." A sudden gust of August wind rattles through the poplar leaves. Cacophony, then stillness. Zoey leans her cheek against the smooth grey stone that marks her mother's resting place and gently runs her fingers across the inscribed words: *Beloved Mother.* "I miss you, Mom," she whispers. "I wish you were still here. I wish you'd known about my baby. Maybe you could have helped. I was all alone and just so scared and he said I had to hide it. I fucked it up so bad! And now I might never get another chance." She gathers up a handful of fallen crimson leaves. She makes a fist around them but they are still too moist to crumble. She strews them around her mother's grave.

On her way home she stops at Dairy Queen and orders takeout. Alone in her own kitchen she spreads the bounty on a handsome plate. It is not a fancy Eli-dinner but it will do her nicely. Chewing and swallowing is not such a chore after all. She wonders who he will find to feed when she is gone, whose kitchen he will use. Maybe Lori will let him cook in his own home, or he might have to find another place or else he'll have to give it up. He wouldn't be the first to have to give up something that he really loves.

171

regrets

The final night in her mother's house, Jerry has been licking her all over. First he licks and then he sucks. Then he spreads her toes apart with his fingers and holds each foot like a hand in his. Zoey giggles. "That tickles!"

His lashes brush her toes. "Do you think you might remember this?"

"I solemnly swear to remember how you sucked my toes."

He rests his head on her knee. "Because I want you to have something special to remember when you think of me."

"Come up here," she orders but he shakes his head so Zoey slides down the bed until she is beside him. She tries to meet his eyes but he turns away. She clambers over his body and again he turns.

"Please don't," he says. "I can't look at you right now."

"You're crying!"

Jerry sniffs. "Who says?"

"I say," says Zoey. "Tell me why."

"Because I'm sad. Because you're leaving me."

"I've been thinking . . ."

"About what?"

"Us. You and me."

"What have you been thinking about us?"

"I thought what if you came back with me? Like to Vancouver."

"You mean it?"

"Yeah. Get away from here. From Eli and the shit about the company. You could stay with me for a bit and then see your folks in Victoria."

"Does this mean there is an *us*, as in together?"

"All I'm saying," Zoey says cautiously, "is that you could come out to the coast with me. I'm talking about a holiday, not a marriage."

"I wouldn't ask for marriage. No promises, okay?"

"If you want to stay for a week, that'd be totally cool with me."

"I wonder," Jerry says, "if you know that I'm in love with you?"

"You know what else I have been thinking?"

"What?"

"I've been thinking how keen it would be to know someone who wouldn't leave me for a change. To know someone who cared enough to stick around."

"Hey!" protests Jerry. "Wait a second! First you tell me no commitment and now you're saying this. What's going on?"

She shrugs. "I was just sharing my wishful thinking." All the promising in the world doesn't change the fact that sooner or later everyone dies or leaves. Her father had promised to love and protect her mother for better or for worse, but he fucked off and she died so what difference do vows make? Besides, the people who you truly love are not the ones who love you back. "I just wonder what it would be like. But I don't think I'm really ready for commitment yet."

"Like I said, no promises."

"Good," says Zoey. "Because I can't give you any. Besides, I'm different when I'm out there; it could turn out that you don't even like me. So, will you come or not?"

"If you're absolutely sure . . ."

"I am. I hate to fly alone."

Before the alarm rings on Sunday morning Zoey extricates herself from the blankets. She goes into her mother's bedroom. Sitting on the upholstered chair beside the window she looks both out and in. Someday she will sell this place but letting go needn't happen all at once. One thing at a time. When Mother died this house was the only security she had to offer other than her insurance policy, but before her illness she was planning to put it on the market and move back to Winnipeg so Zoey could go to university and live at home. Therefore letting go of it would not betray her memory.

While she's pouring cereal the phone beside her rings and she picks up, cradling the receiver on her shoulder. "Hi there El," she says, reaching for the milk.

"How did you know it was me?"

"I was wondering when you'd call."

"So you're going back?"

"Yup."

"Jerry too?"

Zoey crunches cereal. "What's it to you?"

"I knew it! Now that he's finally got his paws on you, he'll be stuck to you forever."

Zoey sighs. "You know El, this is not your business. You gave up all your rights. Is snooping the only reason that you phoned?"

"I'm not prying, I'm asking as a friend. How are you getting to the airport?"

"Okay *friend*, if you must know, his brother is driving us."

"Because I thought I'd offer. We could take the 911 for old times' sake. I'm selling it, you know."

"What would Lori say?"

"I'm missing you already."

"Get used to it."

"It won't be easy."

"I guess you'll have to work at it."

"All I am to you is someone to write letters to who won't write back. Big loss."

"I wish . . ." Zoey stops and loads more cereal on her spoon.

"What?" His voice is eager.

"I was just going to say something dumb. Like I wish you could have loved me."

"I've never been that big on love. I don't think I get it."

"I know, you worry about the other stuff. The things you are supposed to have. Job, family, the right cars, that kind of stuff. I don't guess love figures into it all that much."

"Those things are important to me. I don't see what's wrong with it."

"Nothing, unless they're more important to you than people are."

"You know what I wish?" Eli sounds so wistful that her heart almost skips a beat. "I wish that everything could just have stayed the way it was before. If you hadn't gotten pregnant . . ."

"Well . . ." says Zoey slowly.

"Yeah."

"I guess this is good-bye then."

"Yeah."

"You hang up first."

For a moment he is silent. "I just hope you know," he says at last, "that what I said the other night is true. I *have* loved you. I mean I *do* love you. In my way."

"Whatever."

"So . . ."

"Yeah."

"I guess this is good-bye."

Carefully Zoey sets down the receiver. They have been so civilised it hurts. Surely someone should have pulled a gun, someone should have overdosed or slit their wrists, but no. Even dumping her he is predictable. No drama, no fuss, no mess, no stepping out of line. She should awaken Jerry. They've got a plane to catch.

girlfriend

Jean Paul steps off the airport escalator into her arms. "How are you?" he asks, pulling back to look her over.

"I've been better."

"Do they know who did it yet?"

"No, and they never will. She was doing kids and maybe into snuff; christ only knows what else."

"Same old shit," he says flippantly. "Same old Nancy."

"You're very wrong," says George. "This was new. Is that your only bag? Can we get out of here?"

He shoulders his Vuitton, takes her hand and they begin to walk towards the exit. "So," he says pleasantly. "Did she slip or was she pushed?"

"Your guess is as good as mine."

"When I first heard I thought it was a stunt. Free publicity."

"I hate to admit it, but so did I. She was so obsessed with fame and fortune. I was absolutely sure I'd find her basking in the limelight. *Brilliant!* I thought. When they asked me to identify the body I expected to see some total stranger."

Jean Paul glances at his Rolex. "Do you have a suite?"

"No. I've just been using her apartment. We could go there, if you don't mind."

"Let's do it. It's late and I'm too exhausted to hunt around for a hotel."

George keys open the seven locks on Nancy's door and ushers him in ahead. "I'm a little tense about staying here. I keep thinking the murderer might show up. It was probably someone she knew." She kicks off her shoes and perches on the dishevelled daybed. "I don't know how I'll be able to get to sleep."

Jean Paul sits beside her. "If you lie down, I'll rub your back."

So George lies down, pushes up her shirt and tries to focus on his heavy hands. But all she can think about is Nancy. She lifts her head. "JP," she says.

"Yes?"

"I want to know why you hated her. And don't just say it was jealousy over me because it wasn't. Because you and she go back to long before I ever met her."

His voice is tight. "I don't care to talk about it."

"Please," says George. "It's critical to me."

He shifts. "What did Nancy tell you?"

"Nothing. When I asked her, she'd only say that I should talk to you."

"I need to use the bathroom." Abruptly he stands. Soon she hears the toilet flush and he returns to lie beside her. "I was just thinking," he says pensively. "Most likely it's a blessing she was killed. For her own sake, as it were."

"Why would you say that?"

"Because HIV takes longer, with much the same result."

George shivers, tugging up the blanket. "Do you think she was?"

"You must admit the odds are pretty good. With that insatiable blood-lust you found so endearing, and she never seemed overly concerned about safety, neither her own nor anyone else's. You have to agree it was not her top priority."

"No," says George reluctantly. "No, it wasn't."

"I think you should get tested. You were with her at the Gallery that night. You, and that creep Lazarus . . ."

"He never even touched me!"

"But you touched her and he touched her. Use your head! Do you have any idea how many people she was with? Surely you are not as naïve as that!"

"I've never had much sense where Nancy was concerned," George says wearily.

"Amen to that!"

She sits up. "Please! You have to tell me. Who can it hurt? She's dead and I need to know."

"Alright, since you're so insistent. Provided I can trust you to keep this to yourself. Can you do that?" George nods, then holds her breath. Jean Paul sighs. "It all feels like it happened a hundred years ago. I had an encounter with her. I was just a kid, barely in my twenties, fresh from art school and still wet behind the ears. And, for all intents and purposes, practically a virgin."

"Was this encounter sexual?"

He snorts. "Of course! Everything with her always was, wasn't it? We met during the Fringe when both of us were designing sets for cash and, what else is new? I fell for her. I fell hard. Actually, I think I worshipped her at first. She was so stunning and it seemed as though she knew everyone who was anyone despite the fact that she was a few years younger than me." He pauses to rub his stubble. "I desperately need a shave."

George grabs his fingers. "Then what?" she urges.

"Then I discovered what you already know. That it's not that difficult to have her. For anyone to have her."

"So you fell in love with her and she broke your heart?"

"Unfortunately for me, it was not that simple."

"So what did happen? Did she dump you?"

"Not exactly," he says dryly. "If you haven't noticed yet, Nancy's so-called passion for free choice and mutual consent started and ended with Nancy. Her philosophy was purely selfish; she rarely extended the rights she demanded for herself to others. In my case she arranged a special treat. She staged a rape."

George clutches the blanket between damp hands. "Whose rape?"

"Mine."

"How?"

"I had learned about her other paramours in the usual way, by happening upon them accidentally or maybe it was planned, knowing Nancy, and then I discovered her proclivity for blood sports, both of which I found distasteful even then. I was stumbling around awkwardly like the kid I was, trying to extricate myself from our relationship, if you could call it that. Wanting to escape with minimal damage with her fighting tooth and nail to keep me in it. I don't know why. Maybe she wasn't finished with me yet. Or maybe it was just because she had to be the one to call the shots." He shudders. "This is hard for me."

George sets her hand upon his chest but he shakes it off.

"So one night during this time I was staying over, I don't know why except that I was drunk and overtired and my guard was down and she insisted. I've gone through this a million times in my mind. The way I figure it, they secured me while I was unconscious and when I came to, some guy was . . . Well let's just say aside from bondage and some particularly unpleasant variations on your basic sodomy, he also beat me senseless, with her directing the event as though it were a movie shoot. I think she got it all on film. In the guise of art, no doubt."

"Then what?"

"I passed out and when eventually I came to I had been freed, the place was empty and I got out of there as quickly as I could." He pauses. "It's the oddest thing, but I never felt that it was personal. It was symbolic more than anything. It wasn't so much *me* as my rejection of her. She couldn't tolerate being left and this was her way of telling me that she was in control. Even afterwards she made it quite clear she'd take me back. Provided it was on her terms."

"Did you consider pressing charges?"

"Just think of the publicity!"

"I'm so sorry," says George helplessly. "Why didn't you tell me this before?"

"It's unmanly to be raped. There are all those implications. There's just no way a guy can admit to having been sexually assaulted without being held culpable." He stands. "Let's find out where your girlfriend stashed her booze."

Girlfriend. The term evokes an image of tender intimacies, of fondling under weeping willows, of magnolia blossoms and floppy wide-brimmed hats. Pinafores and secret kisses on idyllic summer lawns. It does not apply to George and Nancy. "Don't call her that," she protests.

Jean Paul rummages through cupboards. "Great!" he exclaims in a moment, pulling down a bottle. "Scotch! What would you call her then?"

"I considered her my obsession."

He stoops to pick up something filmy from the floor. Something *Nancy*, red and silky. He slides it across his palm. "I absolutely hate for you to mourn her!" he says softly. "It disgusts me. You know she isn't worth it! Sometimes when someone dies the world is better off. You may as well accept it."

"Don't!" says George. "I can't take attitude right now. You should have told me about this sooner."

"It would not have made any difference to you. It still doesn't. I'd wager all my savings; I'll bet you're just as much in love with her this minute as you've always been."

"It might have helped me understand some things. I could have confronted her."

"To what end? You forgave her everything, all she had to do was breathe in your direction. You're so easy it's pathetic; a few seconds of tongue is all it takes. In fact, I wouldn't be at all surprised to find out she pursued you just to get back at me for rejecting her."

George bristles. "That's not fair!"

"Maybe not, but it seems more than coincidental that right after you and I got together, she suddenly put herself in your path."

"You didn't come out here to console me, did you?" George demands. "Listen to yourself! Even now you're trying to turn me against her. Even though she's dead. It's pathetic!"

He holds up his hands. "Alright, alright! I confess! I wanted to save you from deceit. To force you to hear reason. To acknowledge that she did this to herself! Accident or no, her eyes were open right up to the bitter end. It could have been that she intended to exploit a scene and got in too deep. But somehow I can't fathom Nancy deliberately giving up control of anything and she and that slimy bastard Nino were about to cash in big, so why now? It doesn't make any sense. For those reasons I don't think she planned for this to happen. But she must have known that she was playing with the big boys and the big boys play for keeps."

George swallows whisky and then sets the bottle between her knees. "What you say makes sense but I don't care. All I know is that no one, absolutely no one had the right to take her life. I know her philosophy was flawed but I also know I loved her, and I can't just erase those feelings with reason. Besides, I believe she was as much a victim of her circumstance as anyone. She tried to make the most of what she had and at least she did it with a certain class."

"As usual you're much too generous," Jean Paul says. "Every single one of us has some cross to bear, but most of us take responsibility for our own behaviour and its consequences. Except sociopaths like Nancy."

"But she did take responsibility!" George says. "Even more than most! Because her life was so completely out of sync with the mainstream she was always conscious of it. Not that she apologised, she just couldn't understand how what's considered 'normal' could be so incompatible with the life she had experienced. She couldn't figure out why people accept the fiction of normalcy as reality when it's so obviously not. Responsibility for actions! You should talk! What about your own behaviour, like the way you constantly remind me of what you think I owe you? You seem to feel that it's acceptable, but it hurts me every single time you say it."

"How can you even compare the few harmless joking comments I may have made with the damage she has done?"

"You're the one who's preaching about taking responsibility for the impact of your actions. Whatever Nancy was, and I'm not saying that I think she was right, but at the very least she tried to be honest about it."

"So now you're accusing me of dishonesty? What about your dishonesty with me?"

"Like what?"

"Like pretending you were interested in marriage. Like not telling me about having been with Nancy when you were."

"I never swore fidelity. Nor did I ever promise to confide every sordid little detail of my life to you."

Jean Paul tugs at the bottle. "Not in so many words," he mutters.

"Not in any words! And anyway, I told you I'd been with her. And with Zoey. When you returned from Paris. I never promised we'd be married, I only agreed to consider it. What do you think I owe you now?"

He sets the bottle on the floor. "Stop it," he grunts.

"If you don't like what you're hearing, you force me to shut up?"

"I mean it!" he shouts and for the first time ever she is afraid of him. "I've taken more from you . . ." And then he's looming over her, shoving her, twisting her arms up, snapping Nancy's bedpost cuffs around her wrists, pushing into her.

She is trapped but she can scream and so she does. Quickly he stuffs her mouth with something soft, Nancy's red silk underwear. She probably bought it on their shopping spree. George gags and spits and spits but she cannot dislodge it. Her bound hands are useless to her. Her mouth is scraped and dry. *Jean Paul,* she wants to plead, *it's me. We don't do this to each other.* But the cloth has silenced her and so she does the begging with her eyes.

After he is spent she is afraid that he will fall asleep and then she will be stuck. Her mouth is stuffed with silk, proving anything can be a weapon when you need one, even splendid underwear. Violently she wrenches back and forth. Whisky, pent-up rage and travel have made him dull but finally he rolls off and tugs out the makeshift gag. "JP," she croaks, "please undo my hands. I have to pee."

He releases her not speaking and she slides from the bed, makes her way to the toilet on her hands and knees. Roaches sprint around her while she fills the rust-stained clawfoot tub with water and a splash of Nancy's soothing oil. Any imaginings she may have entertained of eventual security with him have now evaporated. She cannot lie beside him so she tugs out a rolled futon, removes a pillow he's not using, and sets herself in a corner of the room where she falls asleep, hugging images of Nancy in red leather strutting through her dreams.

182

accessory

Jean Paul steps dripping from the shower. Knotting a scarlet towel around his waist he peers at his reflection. Feathering hair with his fingertips, rubbing knuckles across his chin. To George seated on the toilet, this distinguished greying man bears scant resemblance to the one she encountered here last night.

"I have to leave today," he says briskly. Droplets trickle from his head and come to rest on his neck and shoulders. "Why were you sleeping on the floor?"

George stares at the mirrored man. After what you did, she thinks. "I couldn't sleep with you," she answers.

"Was I snoring?"

George pulls up her panties and stands behind him. "I couldn't sleep with you because of what you did to me last night," she says, meeting his eyes in the misty glass. "Don't you remember?"

He raises his eyebrows. It has a nice effect. "What I did?"

"I'd call it assault."

"As I recall, we had sex."

"You had sex; I was bound and gagged."

He groans. "So this is how it happens! This is how we go from mutual desire to charges and accusations; this kind of misinterpretation. I thought you liked what we were doing."

"You were doing it. I did not consent. Therefore I consider it assault."

Jean Paul spins around. "Let me see your bruises," he demands. "Assault leaves scars. Where are they?" He sets hard hands upon her shoulders.

"Please don't," says George, stepping quickly back.

"Since when has touching you become a crime?"

She bites her tongue. "I'm going to make coffee."

He follows her into the kitchen and watches as she rummages noisily through cupboards. "What are you looking for?" he asks at last. "Evidence?"

"Coffee," she mutters.

He strides to the fridge, opens it and pulls out a can. "Here it is, ground and fresh. I'll make it while you get dressed."

Deciding what to wear is easy since she only brought the clothes upon her back. She smells coffee brewing and her belly rumbles. Nancy's things scattered all about remind her of the corpse she saw, perfect yet deliberately scarred. Her broken body like her art, larger than life itself, both beautiful and horrible. She returns to the kitchen, unfolds a chair and waits for him to set the steaming mug in front of her.

"About last night . . ." he says.

"You don't have to . . ."

"I'm sorry if I hurt you. I think talking about the past triggered something. And being here in her apartment. Honestly, I thought you were enjoying it. After all, you did it rough with her."

Hands trembling, she sets down her mug. "What makes you think I did?" Her voice is high and tight.

"It's obvious! Knowing Nancy." He sounds smug.

"What about knowing me?" asks George. "She and I wanted different things. Mostly she went elsewhere to meet those needs."

"If you say so," he replies. "But you can't blame me for the assumption. At any rate, what I did was done in play."

"Next time ask the person you think you're playing with for their consent before you start."

"I'm sorry," he says. "It was just a simple misunderstanding. At least you aren't hurt."

"I could say thank you," says George. "For helping me decide about this marriage business."

"I'm afraid to ask."

"It's over."

"Ah, yes." He sighs, frowns, then pauses to rearrange his face. "In that case, there are two things I want from you. First, I want you to get tested for HIV and tell me the result. And second, I want you to promise it'll be me you call when next you want a man to bed. Agreed?"

"You can go get tested! I won't be your scapegoat. You're as informed as me; it's up to you to protect yourself. And don't expect me to call on you for servicing; I want someone I trust."

"A game gets a little out of hand and you're withholding trust? That's ridiculous!"

"It doesn't mean we can't be friends," George says wearily. "But I need time to grieve. Without your attitude."

"Even dead she comes between us."

"If that's the way you choose to see it."

"How else should I see it?"

"It's not Nancy, it's you. Aside from what you did last night, not bothering to ask me for consent, your constant comments about my debts to you and the freedom that you promise but won't deliver . . . All these are obstacles to me."

"I still want to spend my life with you."

She shrugs. "Once Nancy told me I had no right to claim I loved her unless I could say I loved all of her, including the parts I didn't like. As far as she was concerned, her rage was just as much a part of her as was her beauty."

"Are you saying that I'd try to change you?"

"Just the bits of me that you don't like."

"I've always said that I'm prepared to overlook your flaws."

"Flaws as defined by you, you mean. But it's what you'll expect from me in return that worries me. What will it be?"

He fills her mug, then his, and offers her the sugar. "My expectations are so simple. I need a wife."

George stirs her coffee. "Tell me what that means to you."

"Someone to be at my side; someone who'll help me care for Mother; someone to grow old with; someone to enrich my life."

"An accessory?"

"In a way."

"Choosing someone to get old with has always seemed to me a touch absurd."

He rubs his fingers across his wrinkled forehead. "Everybody needs companionship."

"There are other ways to get it."

"I don't have a lot of friends. I've neither had the time nor the inclination."

"So a wife would take the place of friendships you haven't bothered to develop."

"It's not unusual," he retorts.

"Men using women to fill their emotional needs?"

"There's nothing wrong with marriage with a friend."

"But marriage instead of friendship . . ."

"I've focussed my energy on my career. So now I have more to offer."

"We always talk in parallels." George shakes her head. "I'm wasting time. I have to get to work. I have to pack this stuff and get it to Vancouver. I need to get it done."

"Are you keeping everything?"

"Of course, it's all archival. Someday a Nancy garter belt will be worth big bucks."

"You do have a practical streak! I've always admired that." He carries the carafe to the sink and rinses it. "You need not accompany me to the airport, I'll just grab a cab. We'll talk about this after you've calmed down, once you're home. When life has returned to normal. Just be sure to save a piece of pricey lingerie for me, alright?"

lust & cobwebs

If she thought packing clothing would be easy, she thought wrong. There is no part of it that doesn't hurt. One after another she fills shipping boxes with neatly folded stacks of fabric, unlaundered. She'll look later, once she is at home, after she's had time to think. Here is the sundress Nancy wore shopping, here's the leather skirt she showcased at the Gallery with stockings stuffed inside as though both were stripped from her body in a single fluid motion; George can see her doing it. If Nancy had been killed three months ago, this task of clearing out would be someone else's responsibility. Unrequited lust for Zoey, a common nightmare, some momentary insecurity with vodka on a rain-filled weekend combined to lead her to a New York morgue and this apartment after half a year of trying to eradicate Nancy from her life.

After clothing she moves to cosmetics. Smell is the most fundamental human sense, no intellectual processing is required for it. One sniff of Nancy's perfume and she is transported back. To the first thrill of knowing she could have the amazon; to the final humiliation of realising she could never be enough. Knowing she would always have to share. And the more George tried to pull her to herself, the harder Nancy pushed her away until one day she just exploded. Then, remorseful or afraid, she took George damaged to Emergency where they sewed her up and reset her bones. While she mended she told anyone who asked that she had been assaulted by a stranger she could not identify.

When love twists into a torment the only options are to somehow make it stop or consent to live or die with it. So George ended their relationship. Afterwards whenever she and Nancy met, George moved as far from her as quickly as she could. The musty cobweb of attraction which wove between them seemed elemental as a scent. It was sexual and caused by pheromones or perhaps unfinished business from another incarnation but George could not distinguish cold hard lust from hot true love where Nancy Rider was concerned; she knew that it was dangerous for her to get too close. For more than half a year she stood firm ground. What she cannot understand is how any time could have dimmed her memory. She must have been blinded momentarily, frustrated by her lust for Zoey who she thought of as a child and unnerved by Jean Paul's repetitive persuasions. She should have remembered all of it.

With Jean Paul there are no fists, there is no rage nor much passion either. She has been safe with him till now. With the contracts that are his style. With his conversations in which the words *I love* are closely followed by words like *I must, I have to* and *I need*.

She will take these cosmetics home. They are the closest thing to Nancy she will ever get again.

sorry

During the flight Jerry chatters on and on about the view, and landing for a stopover in Calgary, he even raves about the Saddledome. He is enthralled by scenery, grass and trees, sky and mountains, and in Vancouver he adores the dogged drizzle. "You'll get bored with it," Zoey warns. "That's one thing you can count on."

George is not waiting at the terminal. After checking with the Information clerk and searching for awhile, Zoey's forehead crinkles. "Something major must have happened for her not to show. Man! That downer really wiped me out. I say let's get a cab." They load their bags into the trunk, then she climbs into the back seat where she can doze while Jerry eagerly clambers in beside the driver to ogle the lush surroundings.

The house is closed and dark. "It looks deserted," Zoey says digging out her keys. "No George to meet us at the airport, Jean Paul's not here . . . This is just too spooky."

"Is he usually at home on Sunday?" Jerry asks.

"I don't know. But it is weird that George wasn't at the airport after she called specifically to ask about the flight." She shrugs and pushes the door open. "Oh well. Grab that suitcase and follow me."

Jerry whistles at the view through the floor-to-ceiling window that overlooks the bay. "I thought artists were supposed to survive on gruel and live in rat-infested garrets."

"As far as I can tell Jean Paul is a famous painter and he's not exactly poor. My room is in the basement. Come on! And bring some stuff."

He follows her downstairs, her big suitcase bumping on his knee at every step. "I'm gonna have a bruise," he complains. "What's in here anyway?"

Zoey turns on a lamp and tosses her arms expansively. "This is it!"

she crows. "It's my very own!" Stretching out her arms she bounces onto the bed. "Check out my waterbed!"

"I should call my mom," he says. "Let her know I'm here."

"I don't have a phone but you can use Jean Paul's. Upstairs, through the door and to your right. It's in the room with all the windows. And make yourself at home. He keeps beer in the fridge, you can help yourself. I think I'll take a nap."

"Just wait." Jerry seats himself on the bed, tugs out a joint, lights and passes it to Zoey.

"I don't think I should," she says. "Not on top of Valium."

"You don't plan to operate a motor vehicle, do you?" She returns the reefer and lies back drowsily, slipping fingertips across his cheek. "You know what I really want?" he asks softly. "I'd like to fuck with you on the beach."

"I haven't done that yet," says Zoey.

"Wow! So I could be your first!"

She reaches lazily to undo his belt. Then she shuts her eyes and waits. It seems a lifetime since George sucked her off on this very bed. Jerry climbs on top, but nothing happens.

"I'm sorry," he whispers, rolling off and pulling up his jeans. "I'm tense, that's all. It's the excitement. The travelling. No sleep. You know."

Yawning, Zoey tugs up the blanket. "I'm passing out. Why don't you just go upstairs and call your mom?"

things change

It takes a minute to recognise her surroundings and another to figure out who's asleep beside her. The bedside clock glows seven-forty. She squints, trying to remember if the lit red dot means day or night. They arrived at dinnertime and she doesn't feel as though she's slept a night so it must be evening. She hears footsteps overhead and in a moment, Jean Paul at the stairwell.

"Zoey!" he calls down. "Are you home?"

Suddenly she feels giddy and a little frightened. "Yeah," she shouts. "I'll be right up!" She flings off the blanket and scrambles to the bathroom to splash her face. She tugs on a shirt, dashes up the stairs and throws her arms around him.

"Where have you been?" he scolds. "George was sick with worry."

"But I talked to her on Thursday."

"That's odd, she never mentioned it," he says. "It must have slipped her mind with all that's happened. So how are you?"

"Fine, I'm great! Also I brought a guest. I didn't think you'd mind."

"Eli?"

"Nope. Jerry, Eli's partner and my old friend from school. He won't be here very long; he's going to go see his folks in Victoria. He's sleeping now."

"Come talk to me," Jean Paul says and Zoey follows him into the living room where they sit together on the couch. Casually he spreads a long arm behind her. "Now," he says, "tell me every detail."

"Well, obviously I went back home. And me and Eli broke up, finally. For good this time."

"What about the guy downstairs? A new paramour?"

"It's a long story."

"I've got all night," he says, brushing her hair with gentle fingertips.

Zoey moves away, pushing off his roving hand. "Don't," she says. "Where is George? She was supposed to meet me at the airport."

"You mean you haven't heard?"

"Heard what?"

He drops his hand on her shoulder and pulls her close. "Someone died."

"Not George!"

"No, of course not! It was Nancy."

"Nancy? The artist? What happened?"

"Her throat was slit. In New York. George is there right now."

Zoey throws off his hand, jumps up and paces from the fireplace to the balcony. "Oh man! This is really bad! Georgie must be heartbroken."

"It's not as grim as you might think. She just stayed on a bit to take care of things."

"But is she heartbroken, or what?"

"I think 'or what.' She'll get over it."

"Get serious! Someone you know is murdered and you act as though it's nothing."

"Nancy had it coming to her. No one I know could possibly have deserved it more."

"But what about George? You must feel something for her, at least. She was in love with Nancy. You do know that, right? It's not some big secret is it?"

"Obviously not," he says dryly, patting the sofa. "Why don't you sit down?" he says. "You make me tense."

Zoey perches gingerly, as far from him as possible. "How is she really?"

He reaches out and sets his hand on her knee. "She's not herself. It seems this whole affair has upset her equilibrium."

Again she moves away. "You're not being very kind."

"Let's face it." Jean Paul smiles. "I'm not the least bit sorry that she's gone and I won't pretend I am. Nancy has a nasty way of bringing out the worst in me; I just can't help it. Why are you so distant? Come closer, I won't bite! Unless of course you want me to."

"Is something going on that I don't know about? Did you and George split up?"

He grasps her elbow with one hand and quickly shoves the other up her thigh. "Why don't you just relax? I only want to touch you!"

"I don't think it's right. And besides, you told me I wouldn't have to do anything with you if I lived here. You promised me."

"Oh christ! You women are all the same! Things change, don't you understand? Don't think so much; just let me hold you for a second. You would not believe how much I've missed you!"

For a second, Zoey thinks of packing up to move again. Then she leans back and parts her legs.

"There you go," he says, bearing down. "That's so much better! Now, doesn't this feel good?"

voices

Jerry climbs the stairs to meet the famous painter in whose home he will be staying. Over the butcher-block island in the kitchen he can see it all spread out. Twinkling freighters scattered in the bay and beyond them rugged shoreline. City neon reflected in black water. Zoey sprawling on the couch, legs apart, head tossed back, smooth throat bare. Nestled in the butcher block are chef's knives, a row of them. Jerry caresses one and then another of their handles. Smooth oiled wood, clean steel blades. Mesmerised he watches, hears her mewing and her gasping and her crying out. If he didn't know better, he would swear she was being hurt. The old man keeps at her and up she starts again.

He should go downstairs to have a shower. He stinks from travel, smoke and fucking. He wills himself to move his feet, but one step at a time seems to take forever. Not that anyone can hear him, not with all the noise she is making. In her bathroom he fiddles with the taps to figure out how they work; he is in home design and has seen every bathroom gadget ever made in North America. The water is soft and salty, he scarcely needs soap to make a lather. They will hear that he's awake now and make themselves presentable. He will forget what he has seen, pretend that he's heard nothing. He wraps himself with a towel, opens up his suitcase for a pair of jeans and clean white tee. He knots his shoulder-length black hair into a ponytail. He has used up fifteen minutes, they must be done by now.

Loudly he walks up the stairs. The front room is lit by candles now showing Zoey primly seated on the couch. The grey-haired man is crouched upon the floor fidgeting through a CD stack. "Hi," says Jerry.

"Did you sleep?" Zoey asks before turning to Jean Paul. "Hey JP, this is my friend Jerry. He's an architect."

Jean Paul presses play and stands, his hand held forward. The two move warily toward each other and grip the way men do when first they meet. "Jerry! Welcome to the very best our country has to offer."

Jerry smells Zoey on that polished hand. "Thanks. I thought I'd take a walk to get my bearings. Do either of you want to come with me?"

Zoey jumps up. "Just let me change my clothes and run a brush across my scalp." Her voice is hoarse.

"So. You listen to a lot of jazz?" Jerry asks when she has gone.

"It's the only music I can tolerate," Jean Paul answers smoothly.

"Somehow I can't imagine Zoey getting into this. She's a techno nut; she likes a beat."

"Are you and she an item?"

Jerry shrugs. "I wouldn't go that far. We're friends. We've known each other since grade school."

"Are you lovers?"

"Friends can be lovers too; it doesn't have to mean any more than that."

"Of course, you're right. It's nice that way, don't you think?"

"You're her boss's boyfriend, right?"

Jean Paul shrugs. "Used to be."

"You've broken up?"

"I'm not exactly sure. She's in New York right now. A woman we both knew was murdered there this weekend."

"That's too bad."

"Yes, it is. But it's caused George to have a minor change of heart about our engagement. It's probably her grief that's talking; we'll have to wait and see."

Zoey bounds into the room. "Let's go," she says. "JP, are you coming?"

He shakes his head. "I've got some things to do. Take your keys. I might be asleep when you return."

"This way," says Zoey once they are outside. "Here, hold my hand."

"Did you wash?"

"What?"

"I said did you wash your hands?"

Zoey shrugs. "Well yeah, I washed."

"Okay, then take me to your famous ocean."

The tide is in, the wind is up and foamy waves splash the shore. "The first time I saw low tide I didn't know what happened. It was creepy. All this stuff that's usually under water was stretched out in the open. Rocks and driftwood, moss and seashells. It was twilight with no one else around. It was like I'd landed on a different planet."

"It reminds me of the Whiteshell. Let's just sit here and listen to the water."

"We could go to the beach. It isn't far. These rocks are slimy."

He strips off his jacket. "Use this," he offers.

Zoey spreads the denim on a rock and seats herself while Jerry settles, knees apart, behind her. "Mmmm," she hums. "You're nice and warm."

"What's with you and this old artist guy?" he asks softly.

"Nothing!" Zoey's voice is sharp.

"So what I saw before was nothing?"

Zoey shoves her chin into her collar. "What you saw?" she asks.

"When I woke up, I noticed you were gone. Then I heard voices so I went upstairs. I thought I should meet my host."

"Oh."

"So? What was that about?"

"Nothing," she repeats. "I don't know. Maybe he was glad to see me."

"You couldn't just hug him or shake his hand? You had to fuck him? Is that the way it's done out here?" A dog splashes past. Then branches crackle above them on the path. "You should know I hate surprises," says Jerry solemnly. "Who else is there?"

"You want a list? Everyone I have fucked by name?"

"Only those you might be fucking while I'm here."

"Just George."

When Jerry stands, she is abruptly cold. "Your boss?" he asks. "His girlfriend?"

"Goofy, isn't it?" She giggles tightly. "Don't I know it!"

"So LJ was right. Are you going to keep on with both of them?"

"I didn't plan it out, it just happened. At first George told me we were finished because I was too young for her, or so she said, but it was actually because she wanted to get back with Nancy. But then she changed her mind about it anyway, and now that Nancy's dead . . . I have no idea where I stand with her. And about JP, I swear it only happened once. I don't know why, he just insisted, but when I moved in here he promised me I wouldn't have to. It wasn't part of our arrangement."

"It's your body; it seems to me you should be in charge of it."

"No one is making me do anything!"

"It sounds to me like they've been using you."

"But mostly I enjoy it."

"All this is way too twisted for an ordinary guy like me. The highlight of my sex life up to now is the threesome you and me had with Eli."

Zoey looks west to open sea. "Maybe I am being used. But I guess it's what I'm used to. And the way I look at it, at least this time I'm having fun."

Jerry sighs and sits back down. Once more he rings his arms around her. "It doesn't have to be like that. It really doesn't. Being fucked around is not the only way of being loved."

"Name me one person who isn't being used, I double-dare you. Eli uses Lori just like Lori uses him. Jean Paul uses George and vice versa. It sounds to me like Nancy was a great big user too. I don't think anyone knows how to love anyway, so you might as well just get your kicks wherever you can find them."

"Maybe this sounds selfish, but where do I fit in? I don't feel like sharing you with all these people. They're rich and famous and I can't compete with them."

"I warned you," she says unhappily. "I told you I was different out

197

here. Before this I've only had one lover. And he convinced me I was frigid. Well, I've proved him wrong."

"You're not chained to someone just because they made you come."

"Do you think it's sick, the part about my being with a woman?"

Jerry runs a finger down her cheek. "To tell the truth," he says, "and besides my jealousy, it kind of turns me on."

"Eli thinks it's revolting."

"I'm not Eli."

"Good, I'm glad! Should we walk some more?"

"Make me a promise?"

"It all depends."

"Promise me you'll let me know when I should leave. Before I've outstayed my welcome."

"Sure," says Zoey. "And I always try to keep my promises."

fingering in first class

Get everything together in the same place, that seems to be the key. She makes arrangements for the shipping and delivery of Nancy's things. Nino is in charge of arranging for the transportation of the body and the funeral. He has also told her that there is a will, its reading is scheduled for next week and she should attend. Proof maybe that Nancy considered her more than just another notch.

Before she leaves New York the police ask her questions but she won't be the one to give them information. People who knew Nancy know what happened and those who didn't have no right to. The father who is responsible is dead and gone already and there's no one left alive to hold accountable.

Flying back to Vancouver, George wonders if they've stashed the body on this plane. She and Nancy have done this trip before, cunnilingus in the can and fingering in first class under the haze of too little sleep and too much shopping. Nancy liked to travel east to west because it made her younger. Age-obsessed, she used to try to calculate how long it would take to bring her age down to zero. But now there is no need for magic formulae, she has been stopped in time. She will be forever thirty-six. George tugs out her pen and pad to begin the eulogy.

She arrives early Monday. Takes a taxi home and falls into her bed exhausted. She doesn't even check her messages. The funeral is being planned for Sunday. It would have been Nancy's thirty-seventh birthday.

skinny girls

Zoey skips work on Monday. Instead she takes Jerry on a walking tour and they stop for lunch on Granville Island.

George sleeps in till dinnertime. She needs to be at Nancy's to accept delivery, but she doesn't want to go alone so she calls Jean Paul.

"You're home already?" he asks.

"Yes, I'm home," she says coolly. "Barely. Is Zoey there?"

"Yup, she's back. She brought some guy along."

"Eli?"

"Nope. His buddy Jerry. Cute kid. Looks like he could barely wait for the ink to dry. But I think he's the consolation prize."

"Get her on the phone."

Carrying the cordless to the stairwell, he shouts down. "Zoey! Phone! It's George."

Two steps at a time she dashes up. "Hiya!" she says breathlessly. "How are you?"

"Alright. Considering."

"I heard about what happened and I don't know what to say. I'm really sorry."

"Thanks. I have to go to Nancy's house to meet the courier. Will you come with me?"

"Sure! I can hardly wait to see you."

"I'll be there in ten minutes. We'll order pizza."

"Cool!" Zoey tosses the phone on the counter and races down the stairs.

"What's up?" asks Jerry.

"I'm off to Nancy's house with George." Zoey scrambles into her jeans.

"Maybe you could catch a movie. Ask JP to go."

"How long will you be gone?"

She tugs up her zipper and drops onto the bed beside him. "Look," she says. "George has way more important stuff on her mind than diddling me. She doesn't want to be there waiting for the courier alone. And JP never got along with Nancy so she won't ask him." Leaving Jerry sucking reefer and staring at the ceiling, she hurries up again to wait outside for George's clunky Volvo. When it pulls up, she races to it.

George leans across the seat to open the passenger door. Her eyes seem bruised, her hair's unwashed and she's showing wrinkles Zoey's never seen on her before. "Get in," she says.

Zoey pecks the air around her face. "You look fabulous!"

"Never mind the bullshit. I look like hell." George pushes on the gear shift to manipulate her car around the tired silver Saab permanently parked in front of Jean Paul's house. "But thanks for lying anyway."

"Okay, so I admit you look a little wasted. But who could blame you?" Their destination is a shabby little house in the West End cut off from street view by old trees. George parks the Volvo and turns off the ignition while Zoey peers out through her window. "She should get someone to caretake while she's away like I do. It's all overgrown."

"Tidiness was the last thing on her mind," says George, opening her door. "She was never big on tidiness."

Zoey follows her down the path. "But if the yard is cared for, it looks like someone's home. Cops claim it fools burglars."

George snorts. "No robber could find anything to steal in this house. They'd have to clean it first." On the stoop, she digs around for the keys. The deadbolt lock is sticky and she has to wiggle it until finally it catches. Then she pushes the door open and Zoey steps in first. George follows, flicking on the overhead.

Clutter litters every surface. Unruly piles of paper, bottles and containers, plastic mixed with glass, swatches of fabric and heavy vinyl, patterns cut in pieces and then scattered.

Zoey picks a cautious path across the room. "It's so weird to be where someone famous lived."

"Jean Paul is famous," George points out. "And you're living in his house."

"First of all, he isn't dead. And secondly, he seems like any other guy. But he sure is a better housekeeper!" At the kitchen doorway, she stops stock-still. Then slowly she turns. "You don't want to look at this right now," she warns, stretching out her arm.

"Come on," says George. "We'll wait outside. I'll phone for pizza on the cell."

Settling on a step, she calls in an order and then begins to comb through Zoey's hair. "Did I ever mention Nancy had a thing for redheads?" she asks softly. "It's a good thing she never met you; she would have eaten you right up. So tell me, who's this Jerry guy?"

"Just a friend from home. He thinks that he's in love with me."

"What happened out there anyway?"

"Eli's wife found out. She's pregnant, they're married, she wins."

"What about your house?"

"I hired an agency to look after it, to make sure the furnace works and the eaves are clean, check on it from time to time, stuff like that. It doesn't cost a lot. I sorted my stuff out too, but I still haven't decided what to do with the house or my life. My mother wanted me to go to university."

"You could do that here."

"I could do that anywhere." She jerks her head. "Please stop playing with my hair! But I don't think I'll stay in JP's basement though."

"Why? Is something wrong?"

"He's been coming on to me and I don't want him to."

A van pulls up and George digs around in her bag for her wallet.

"You gals call for pizza?" the driver asks, bouncing up the path toward them.

"Yup." Zoey eyes him appreciatively. Nice smile. Firm butt. No wedding band.

George takes the box and pays. Cheerfully the boy makes change for her and winks at Zoey before he bounces off. George taps her shoulder. "Here," she says. "Careful. It's hot."

Zoey smirks. "So is he! Did you check out those buns?" The van honks before it pulls away. Zoey stares down at the pizza in her hand and then looks up at George. "I've been experimenting," she says.

"With what?"

"To stop myself from throwing up. I chew each bite fifty times and try to think about how the food I'm eating tastes."

"Throwing up?"

"Yeah. You know, when you upchuck after eating. And sometimes I also binge."

"I never knew."

"That's because I hide it. I've always hidden it. I've been at it ever since my mom got sick. Eli goes for skinny girls, the skinnier the better."

"Maybe you could talk to Smitty," ventures George. "She's a doctor, she knows about this sort of thing. It couldn't hurt."

"I don't do it all the time," Zoey says defensively. "I'm mostly in control."

"I'm not blaming you," says George, looking down into the greasy box. "I know this probably doesn't help the way you feel, but I think you're perfect as you are. Would you like another slice?"

"Sure, thanks. Tell me about Nancy."

"She was into sadomasochism; S&M."

"Isn't that about people beating on each other to get off?"

"In a nutshell. I think someone went too far and now she's dead."

"You mean her throat was slit by accident?"

"Yes."

"Why would she do that kind of shit in the first place?"

203

"I think it was her father's fault. He was very cruel to her, extremely violent."

"Is that the way it works?"

"That's my theory, although a lot of people disagree. Nancy claimed she did it just because she liked it."

"What about you?" asks Zoey. "Did you like it too?"

"Aha!" George says briskly. "There's the courier!"

After they unload and stack the crates inside, she locks up and they get into the Volvo to drive back over the Burrard Street Bridge.

At Jean Paul's house Zoey opens the passenger door. "Should I be at work tomorrow?"

"I'm taking the week off and you have a guest. It seems silly for you to be there on your own. Don't bother."

"Do you really think I could talk to Smitty?"

"Absolutely."

"Then I will." Zoey steps onto the curb. She smiles and waves until the car is out of sight. She's never told a single soul before about the cleansing. Somehow the telling has made her feel lighter. She twirls around the sidewalk, then at once feels silly. After all, she is a grown woman now and grown women should not dance on city sidewalks in plain view of anyone who happens to be looking.

still waters

George sits alone in darkness. Zoey's admission has her thinking about still waters. She has had a feeling, nothing more than something vague, based on the silent concentration during meals, her body far too tiny to be healthy, those mysteriously replaced groceries. Her way of coping with abandonment perhaps. Everyone has something. Jean Paul has his clinging mother, Nancy had her father, Zoey has her losses. Even Nino, scuttling off with Nancy's lifeblood clutched between bloated greedy hands, probably has had something for which to compensate.

Nancy's work was the only thing that truly mattered. The canvases she's left may help make her death less futile and George has decided she will write the story to go with them. It's the least that she can do. She will piece Nancy's life together, using words to paint the portrait of an artist. So Nancy's final gift to her is not that sexy slender whip at all, it is her story. George shudders, overwhelmed with sudden awful fear.

grazing

Zoey lets herself into a silent house and tiptoes to the kitchen. It isn't all that late but Jean Paul beds early and Jerry might be sleeping too. She opens up the fridge, looks in, then closes it. There's not a thing she wants to eat right now but she would like to hold someone who cares.

A key turns in the lock and Jean Paul enters. "Oh, hi," says Zoey, looking past him. "I thought you were asleep already. Is Jerry with you?"

"He went downtown to catch a movie. So I guess it's just the two of us, unless George is here." He purses his lips suggestively. "If you'd like to slip into something more comfortable, let's say my bed, I could be convinced to join you."

Zoey grips the refrigerator door. "I don't think so," she says firmly.

Carefully he sets down his pulled-off boots and in his stockinged feet he walks toward her. When he reaches her, he makes a trap with both his hands against the fridge, one on either side of her. She ducks out underneath and leans against a cupboard.

"What's the matter love?" he asks. "Depressed? Unhappy? Doctor Jean has a cure. Just show me where it hurts."

She clenches her teeth. "I think we need to talk," she says.

Heartily he laughs. "Oh good! A talk! Come with me into my parlour and you can talk your little heart out."

Zoey curls her fingers around the counter top behind her. "I don't want to piss you off," she says tightly. "But I don't want to get cozy with you either. I only have one thing to say. You and me doesn't work. I don't know why it happened except that I was overtired and you pushed me into it."

"I pushed you?" he asks loudly. "You seemed to like it well enough.

Next you'll be calling what we did a rape. What's with the women in my life these days?"

"I didn't say I didn't like it. But you promised me I wouldn't have to if I didn't want to, and I think you might have changed the rules without telling me."

He twists his eyebrows. "Are you saying that I forced you?"

"Not exactly."

"Then what, exactly, is your problem?"

"It felt as though I didn't have a choice."

"Well." Coolly he steps back, surveys his shelves, pulls down a bottle and a glass. Quickly he pours and drinks. "Should I apologise?"

"I'm not saying it's all your fault. I could have said no."

"I swear I'll never do it again." He lifts his fingers in salute. "Scout's honour."

Zoey exhales. "Thanks."

"Is that all?"

"I don't know, I guess I feel confused. About everything. I know I haven't had enough loving in my life, but I think I've also learned something else about myself this summer. I don't think I'm the kind of person who can screw a lot of people just to maybe find it."

Jean Paul pours another drink. "None of us has had enough. We all just muddle through nibbling on each other. I call it grazing; it's the curse of my entire generation. Although some make more of a meal from it than others. Take Nancy Rider, for example."

"Well I'm not in your so-called generation and I'm definitely not into grazing."

"You may think that now, but you're still young. Time has a nasty way of changing one's ideals."

"I don't think so," Zoey says.

"I myself would rather be a feaster. But I haven't found someone to feast with who wants to feast exclusively on me. So either I stay celibate or I graze."

"I thought you wanted George."

"George is not monogamous."

"But with Nancy gone . . ."

"Knock wood! She isn't buried yet!" Hurriedly he raps the cupboard door. "Besides, as you well know, she was only one of a myriad of our mutual friend's sexual distractions."

Zoey leaps to answer the back door for Jerry who is spraying raindrops like a cat. "Man it's wet out there!" he says enthusiastically. "I'm soaked right through!"

Jean Paul laughs. "Hello and good-bye," he says. "I'm off to bed. Goodnight."

"'Night," Zoey echoes absently, touching Jerry's rain-drenched sleeve. "I'll get you a towel."

eulogy

All night till dawn and later George scratches out her words. Long-hand, on paper. Not the typical set of standard phrases with which to mourn and bury, but then Nancy wasn't typical. She writes until bone-weary, crashes and awakens, has coffee and writes some more. She turns off the phone. Finally on Friday she sets down her pen.

On Friday she goes shopping for a trashy dress showing a more than tasteful hint of cleavage. Red slinky satin slit down to the nipples in the front and to the crack in back, matching scarlet gloves snaking over elbows, and sling-back sandal heels. Nancy would approve.

On Saturday she composes a fifteen-minute eulogy.

Sunday is Nancy's thirty-seventh birthday. George checks the horoscope for Virgo. *The full moon on the fourth could activate a domestic crisis that forces you to choose between your role in the world and your home life. Choose the former: that's where the cosmic energy is. After the twentieth, your social life takes on a larger role and you'll be able to relax with friends. Best day for a date: the third. Don't even think of doing anything important on the seventh or the eighth, when the Sun, the Moon, and Pluto are at cross-purposes. Between the thirteenth and the fifteenth, public presentations succeed beyond your wildest dreams and career matters progress beautifully. Sign contracts on the twenty-first.* It's too late for contracts and warnings and wildest dreams come true, and much too late for social life or cosmic energy.

Then she checks Sagittarius. *For once you're making money, but the stars are telling you to focus on others. If you're in a committed relationship, your mate needs attention. If you're seeking partners in love or work, you could find them between the twelfth and the fifteenth, but Venus is retrograde, so don't push. This is an instance where she who dominates is lost.* George shuts the magazine. The limo will be here at noon.

Pre-publicity has been excellent. Naturally there will be lookers-on who could care less about either Nancy or the arts but want sensational tales to brag about to friends over cappuccino, the SM gang in decadent regalia will come to claim her as their own, the suits, agents and collectors, and finally the media in full force. Tabloids sniffing out a bit of scandal for their readers who get vicarious kicks from airbrushed heroes being trampled. Speech tucked securely in her handbag, George checks her makeup one last time and pees so she won't have to do it at the chapel.

As she anticipated, the house is packed. Head high, she walks the aisle while whispers ripple like wild wind across a prairie field, everyone wondering who she is. Behind her, six exquisite pallbearers wearing virgin white wheel in the whitest casket possible. At the front they halt. Then twelve gloved hands in unison raise the lid to reveal Nancy clad entirely in shocking crimson. With the ornate antique silver brace George picked out for her to wear locked about her neck to hide the scar, she looks absolutely sexy. There will be no prayers since Nancy did not believe in God or any other Higher Power so they would be a mockery to her.

George waits her turn to speak with stomach churning and then at last she stumbles up to a rumble of applause. From the podium she gazes down into the casket at the only other splash of scarlet in the chapel. "My sweet, you look divine!" she whispers as the noise dies down. Then somehow she makes it through her fifteen minutes before inviting everyone to join her in the birthday song.

The hand-picked bearers roll the coffin out and George is ushered to a waiting limo. This time she gets to ride with Nancy all the way, no sharing. Mourners sniffle and some sob. The photogenic chain-and-leather gang have scattered but the cameras still roll, recording every precious final moment. Brilliant red blossoms sheath the dirt exposed around the grave into which the body will be lowered. At the gravesite she is flanked by Zoey, Jerry and Jean Paul.

"Lean on me," Zoey whispers as she tucks her black-gloved hand into the crook of George's elbow.

Jean Paul nudges her on the other side. "Outstanding eulogy!" he murmurs. "The dress is fabulous! Perfectly divine!"

After the casket has been lowered, mourners stop by with condolences and thanks to her while the cemetery empties.

"I've made dinner reservations," Jean Paul says. "For all of us. Will you come?"

"Of course," says George. "I'm writing her biography, did you know?" He guffaws. "Finally!" he says enthusiastically. "You'll be making money."

the reading

Nino is already present and so are all of Nancy's lawyers in deeply cushioned chairs. The room is long and sombre, rife with rich mahogany and elaborate with heavy drapery. The man seated at the table's head clears his throat importantly. "Now that we're all here, let's begin with introductions. I am Harold Chapin, the senior partner, and these are Rex Sullivan and John Grey." Solemnly he gestures right and left.

"My name is George," George says.

"And I am Nino," says Nino stiffly. "Agent to the unfortunately deceased."

Harold clears his throat. "This is the reading of the last will and testament of Nancy Rider; its final revision occurred on August seventh of this year and was duly witnessed by myself and Mr. Grey, present here. Ms. Rider says, 'All my paintings and creations, except for the selections noted, shall become the uncontested property of my agent Nino, who I expect will make a killing with them, under the guidance and tutelage of the law firm of Chapin and Sullivan, which I have retained to conduct my financial affairs from now till doomsday. They will also execute the Trust in support of artists which I have established through them. The money will be dispensed annually to five individuals working in the arts by a jury of Nino's choosing. These awards are to be based equally upon potential, merit and need.

" 'My house and all its contents, including art, goes to George. Because I owe you, precious, you know what for. Even if we aren't speaking at my time of death. Aside from the house, where I hope you'll live in prosperity for many years, *without* Jean Paul I might add although I'm not making it conditional, I'm giving you five hundred thousand dollars: because

(a) you deserve it; and (b) based on the principle we've discussed that those who have are given more and I think it's your turn to be a recipient for a change; and (c) to prove you wrong. You don't have to live in poverty to have ethics.'" Mr. Chapin stops reading and nods at George.

"Is that it?" she asks. "May I be excused?"

"The paperwork has been prepared. Check in with the receptionist before you leave."

George tries to stand. *She isn't going to make it*, someone says and then, *This often happens. Bend down, close your eyes . . . Now, breathe.* Eventually she lifts her head. Smoothly Mr. Grey removes his hand. "How are you?"

"Better," she says. "I think I can do this now."

"Here, let me help you out. We could arrange a ride."

"No thanks. I have my car." Six eyes fix on her while he leads her from the room. "Jenny, this is George. You have some documents. The Rider estate."

The receptionist wheels around, smiling broadly. "Is it really you?" she asks. "You're the author?"

George nods. "Could I have some water? I almost passed out in there."

"It happens," Jenny soothes. "You needn't be embarrassed." Pulling a Dixie cup from a dispenser, she fills and offers it. "I have both your books," she says shyly. "You probably hear this all the time, but I think you are truly wonderful! I was so thrilled when I found out I might get to meet you! I brought them in today, just in case. I'd really love to have your autograph!" George grins while Jenny slides a pile of paper across her desk. "Business first."

"What is all this?"

"You get the house, right?"

"That's what they said."

"That's what these are for. Sign beside the red Xs. And this is about a cash endowment, five hundred thousand dollars. Sign here and here. This means the money has been placed in trust for you. Once you've presented these papers to the bank, it's all yours." George signs in triplicate and then Jenny proffers copies of her novels. "This is wonderful!" she sighs. "I've never had a book of mine autographed before! What are you writing now?"

"It's a biography of Nancy."

"I saw you at her funeral on the news. You did a speech or something."

"A eulogy."

"Well, good luck. And thanks a lot! I really mean it!"

George takes the scenic route to Wreck Beach. By now the hawkers and the dedicated nudists have retired to warmer climes. Nancy used to come here with her charcoal and her sketch pad to study form. George parks and climbs down to the shore. The tide is high, the sky is overcast. Now that she has money of her own there is nothing stopping her. She will unearth the mystery of Nancy Rider. And in her heart of hearts she is assured, Nancy would have wanted it this way.

on the payroll

Zoey's first task as research assistant gives her keys, one to Nancy's house and one to the Volvo. She will put to use her housekeeping skills, clean up and search for clues for George's book. Jerry's coming too. "I'll do the upstairs," Zoey tells him, "and you can start down here. If you find something you think might be important, put it to one side. Cleaners will come after we've finished to take care of garbage but George wants us to keep letters, photographs, anything about the past, her childhood, a father or any other family."

Nostrils flaring, Jerry sniffs stale air. "So this is how the famous really live," he says scornfully.

"Not all," says Zoey. The task at hand reminds her of clearing out her mother's things. But Mother was as methodical in death as she was in life. Besides, she had warning and so took care of most of it herself beforehand. She always paid her bills as soon as they arrived, and in her home, food was to be eaten in the kitchen only, with leftovers immediately discarded. She wrote the date of purchase on every eggshell with a felt-tipped marker before she put it in the fridge. Winter clothing was dry cleaned and stored for summer and vice versa. Every tube of toothpaste was used completely and then tossed out before another could be opened. She ran the tightest ship. That was how Zoey learned. She's never even tossed her clothes upon the floor and it appalls her to see it done. Nancy's unopened bills and receipts are scrambled in among her crumpled underwear. Stiff paintbrushes, open cans of solvent, used tampons and filthy laundry cover every surface. Foods half-eaten in nooks and crannies have gone mouldy. Never mind sifting through it, Zoey thinks they should rent a bin, park it by the door and shovel it all in.

How can people live like this knowing someday they will die? Purging has to happen sometime or someone else gets stuck with it. People gather too much muck around themselves. Too much of everything; clothing, cards and received gifts never used or even looked at more than once. Photographs and trinkets, meaningless if they can't be seen or found. Where would someone like Nancy have kept mementos? In a closet? Underneath a mattress? Maybe scattered in the attic or the cellar. Zoey rolls up her sleeves and begins to uncover the famous woman's life. Bondage toys on one pile and undies in another. Paint and art supplies in one corner, books and papers in another.

"This woman was a swine," says Jerry, coming up behind her. "How can anybody live like this? You should see the downstairs! There's roaches! George will have to fumigate if she ever wants to live here."

Zoey wrinkles her nose. "Up here too."

"Also I found condoms. Used. I didn't want to touch them."

"There must be rubber gloves around. Every household has a pair. Those ugly pink or yellow things, you know."

"I've looked, but if they're here I can't find them."

"Usually they're underneath a sink."

"I've checked the kitchen."

"How about the bathroom?"

"I was on my way." He pokes around her stacks. "What do you suppose these are for?" he asks, lifting a gigantic pair of steel tweezers.

"I wasn't sure so I put them on the bondage pile. It figures you would look there first."

"Kinky," he says. "What else is here? Oh man, that's some nasty-looking dildo!"

Zoey shudders. "Why don't you go buy some gloves? There's a store around the corner, they should sell them there."

He tosses down the plastic tube. "Come with me."

"I don't want to interrupt myself; I'm on a roll."

He whistles on his way out and down the path. Zoey cracks her knuckles one by one, then reaches for the next item. A photo album. Idly

216

she flips it open. Naked children, blindfolded, bound and gagged, rows and rows of them in black and white. Some are on all fours. Some are standing up; some are lying down. Some fuck each other. Some look dead. Some are bleeding. Weapon-wielding adults wearing masks and leather tower over them. Other adults wearing masks and harnesses are fucking them. And someone must be taking pictures. But they are only kids! Some are infants. Images of concentration camps leap into her head; images of captured people being violated by their captors.

She stumbles to the bathroom retching uncontrollably and shaking. How could anyone be into that for kicks? How could George have been in love with someone who was? Is she into it too? When she says *S&M* it seems like sugary buds of candy.

The front door slams. "I'm back," calls Jerry. "I brought us lunch."

Zoey splashes icy water into her palms to rinse her face and mouth and manages to make it down the stairs without gagging.

"Gloves," he says holding up two sets, a yellow and a pink. "I decided to get them both."

"That's good," says Zoey. "I can't touch a goddamned thing in here with my bare hands. It's too revolting."

"Grab yourself a sandwich. There's salmon, tuna and egg salad, take your pick."

"I really hope you washed your hands."

"I did."

"With soap?"

"Yes, with soap. How come you're sounding like my mother?"

"I found something really gross."

He wraps his lips around egg salad, bites down and chews. "Another implement?"

"Worse. Pictures of little kids being tortured. In a plain old photo album. The old-fashioned kind, with triangular black stickers on the corners to paste the photos to the pages. Why would anyone do that? Why would they take pictures of it? You think it turns them on?"

Jerry slits into plastic wrapping. "It takes all kinds."

217

"But these are kids, little helpless kids! Some are even babies!" Zoey glares angrily at him. "Would that get you hard?"

"Jesus! Don't take it out on me! They're not my fucking pictures! I'm just here because of you, remember? I don't even know these friends of yours."

"I'm calling George."

"She didn't want us to phone her over every little thing. And we'll probably find a lot more before we're done. Anyway, George knows about her sweetheart's funky habits, doesn't she? Isn't that the point to this?"

"She never mentioned kids."

"Trust me, I think she knows. Put it on a pile and save it."

"I don't want to go back up there by myself."

"There's no reason we have to do it this way, with me down here and you up there. We can work together. Have something to eat and then we'll get to it."

Unfortunately he is right and they do find more of the same. It gets a little easier to not react to every discovery. Pretending they are detectives, his idea, and with the gloves and two of them instead of one alone, day passes into evening.

George phones at nine o'clock. "Have you found anything I can use?"

"Depends what you mean by *anything*," Zoey answers. "Do pictures of kids being tortured count? Or is that nothing?"

"Kids?" George sounds tense. "Are any of them Nancy?"

"I'm pretty sure she's one of the consenting adults. You know, the big ones doing the molesting?"

"Are you angry?"

"Yes, I'm angry!" Zoey yells. "If you knew we'd find these and didn't warn me, then yes I am! I'm mad as hell."

"I wasn't sure what you'd find. I'm sorry."

"I can't believe you loved this creep. Are you into that shit too?"

"You've had enough. It's time to get some air and clear your head."

Zoey slams down the receiver. "I'm walking back," she says loudly.

"What about her car?"

"If she really needs it, she can get it for herself!"

While he secures the door, Zoey mutters. They walk across the busy bridge and then along the shore in silence. Jerry doesn't even comment on the beauty of the water or the anchored ships in the bay. He says nothing at all about the ducks lining up for snacks on the rocks nor the magnificence of the mountains nor the streaming sunset.

"So," says Zoey finally.

"Yeah," he answers.

"What do you think about all of this?"

"I think it's weird. You always sort of wonder. Well, at least I do. You hear about this shit and people being into it and you always sort of wonder if you might end up liking it. No matter how horrible it sounds, who really knows what will make them horny until they see or do it?"

"So? Does it?"

He shudders. "Not at all. It makes me want to hurl."

"Georgie says it has to do with adults who were abused as kids needing to do it to other kids to get off. That's the reason for this so-called research. We're supposed to find some kind of proof that Nancy was molested by her dad. But I'm not sure she's right; I don't think that every single person who was hurt is into it."

When they arrive at Jean Paul's house the sun has set. Dinner has been prepared and is heating on the stove, and the table has been beautifully set with candles. Jerry lights them and then he spreads food on plates. "This is nice," he says. "These psychotic friends of yours have their good points too."

219

love letters

George pokes her head around the doorway, looking like a kid tucked in cozy flannel. "Oh hi," she says. "I thought you were the courier."

"I'm glad to see you too," Zoey says. "Can I come in?"

"Of course. You're just in time for coffee."

Zoey follows George's flopping slippers and then watches her measure grounds from a paper bag. "How's the writing going?"

"I think I've had a breakthrough."

"What happened?"

"When I got back last week, I placed a bunch of ads in papers all around the country looking for people who knew Nancy, and yesterday I got a call from someone who claims to have been a girlhood lover. She says she saved their letters and she even kept a diary; she's sending them by courier today. Thank the gods for scribes; as far as I could tell Nancy never even wrote a grocery list."

"That's fantastic!" Zoey rubs her temples. "I just don't know how much more of this Jer and I can take."

"I tried to tell you the sort of thing that she was into. That's what this book will be about."

"I thought S&M was about costumes. Dressing up, tattoos and getting pierced, everyone does it. It's makeup."

"My god! She was murdered! Her throat was slit! Didn't that tell you she was into more than dressing up?"

"I hate to say it, but maybe she deserved it! I mean what kind of lunatic gets off on hurting kids?"

"Oh honey," says George softly. "I promise you I never knew about the kids. I swear! I would have warned you if I did."

Zoey takes the small step into George's arms. While she sobs, the coffee drips. At last she sniffles and mops her nose. "I don't know what's got into me," she says. "I never cry."

"Don't worry," George says, patting her. "You're under too much stress. By the way, where is your sidekick?"

"Asleep in bed. I guess it's more tiring to investigate the slashing of a porno queen than to design a patio."

George sets two mugs on the table and gestures Zoey to a chair. "Have you talked to Smitty yet?"

Zoey takes a sip and smacks her lips. "You make great coffee."

"Which means you haven't."

"There's so much shit around to deal with that I haven't had the time."

"So," George says briskly. "If you have a second now, here's the phone and there's her number."

The doorbell rings and while George is chatting with the courier, Zoey makes her call. "I made an appointment," she shouts.

"Excellent!" George calls. "Come here and look at this!"

"Is it more of Nancy's crap?"

"Daisy says it's mostly writing. Journals and notes and such. Bring coffee."

Zoey carries the pot with her to the front room where George is tearing wrapping off a box. "Who is Daisy?"

"Nancy's childhood sweetheart. Don't you think that's sweet?"

"It's hard for me to think of Nancy Rider as being sweet."

"Oh come on! Tormented love and adolescent angst! All right here inside this box."

"Don't forget, I'm barely over my own adolescence and it isn't as romantic as you seem to think. Did Nancy ever talk about this Daisy?"

"She never mentioned any names, but she did tell me about a high school crush. I guess it was rare for a girl to have a girlfriend in a prairie town in the seventies. It wasn't done back then."

"Or now."

"Aha!" crows George. "Look at these! High school pictures!"

Zoey scrunches close. "Is that her?"

"I'm pretty sure," says George breathlessly.

"She's so beautiful! You never told me that."

"Oh god, you didn't have to say it, she just was! Even dead she was a knock-out, you saw her! Oh! Oh, oh! Look! Check this out!"

"Jeez Louise! Relax! What is it?"

"Letters. My god, she saved Nancy's letters!"

"Love letters, do you think?"

"What else would they be? Let's see . . . 'My precious flower . . . ' Oh yes! Absolutely!"

"Read me the whole thing."

George takes a breath. "It's a poem," she says. "Okay, here goes."

daisy
soft blossom
petal lips open up
    beneath me
    breathe me
    tongue fastened to me
    i feel red satin white silk
come with me & how
you make me
burn burst & bloom
    sometimes even cry
    wet tears last night i
    dreamed you
    ? can i say perfect perfect perfect ?
you a picture
give to me
forever
    with one (1) kiss
    two (2) smiles
    i am.
    forever nan)

George refolds the tattered paper and tucks it tenderly back into the box.

"Are you sure Nancy wrote that?" Zoey asks. "It seems kind of sappy."

"It's signed 'Nan.' Remember she was just fourteen." George flips rapidly. "Ah-hah!"

"Let me see!"

"They're naughty photos. You might not . . ."

"Shit! Look at that!"

"Here's a note from Nan to Daisy. It says, 'You said you wanted pictures, so here they are. Daddy took these of me in spring. Nan.' Look at these poses, it's kiddie smut! I've got him now, the prick! Evidence in black and white!"

Zoey clutches her abdomen. "I feel sick," she whimpers. "I think I have to . . ."

Hurriedly George pushes down her head. "There," she says. "Think of filling up your lungs, bad air out, good air in. There, that's better. That's good. That's fine."

"I think it's over," says Zoey weakly.

"I don't have to go through this stuff while you're here."

"Don't stop because of me! I'm just wasting time before getting back to work."

"I don't want you at the house today. Take a break, clear your head."

"I promised you I'd do it," says Zoey stubbornly. "Shit like this happens and people have the right to know. They'll read your book because she's famous and telling it might help some other kid."

"I can hire someone else. It doesn't have to be done by you."

Zoey rests her head on George's shoulder. "At least now I understand it better," she says softly, "why you fell in love with her. I've been seeing her as just someone who was into ugly stuff, but she had her good side too. I mean if nothing else, she was really gorgeous."

"She was something else!" George's eyes glisten. "Everyone who met her fell for her."

"I'd like us to make love," says Zoey. "Could we do that?"

When George smiles, Zoey pokes underneath pyjamas. There she tastes sweet nipples, and then she spreads hot pussy lips and sips. Scattered at their feet are images of Nancy's childhood, gentle poems written when she was just fourteen, hope-filled and very much alive.

After Zoey leaves, George dips into the box again. Letter after letter, picture after picture, Daisy's wistful journals. She must have been Nancy's lifeline in those days, a confidante, someone to be honest with about the liberties her daddy took. Someone she could choose to fuck or not, for a change a choice. George fights her rising jealousy, trying to remind herself she never even knew this girl. What she knew was leftovers: blind rage, vicious fists and hostile scenes. What she knew was the end result of first the father and then the SM gang that adopted her when she hit the street at fifteen, cheeky and cocksure, damaged then abandoned, her firm fine body as her only asset. Where she stayed until she started eking out a scrawny living from her sketches. Years of eating macaroni notwithstanding.

She sucks up words written a millennium ago. An injured child who could not forgive herself for having been there in the first place. A toughened kid who struggled for survival in a warped and brutal world; a young girl who seldom got a break. George combs through Daisy's journals for an answer.

Daisy's Journal

April 17th

Me & Nan skipped today and took a long (3 hours) walk by the river. I promised to help her with her math again. 'Daddy' says she has to ace it and whatever 'daddy' wants ... She had more bruises and when I asked her why she takes it, she said I wouldn't understand. She says they 'love each other' & that he only 'wants what's best for her.' What kind of 'best' is that? She tries so hard but it's never good enough. I think beating her turns him on & everything that she does 'wrong' is just another bullshit excuse for him to do it to her. I just want to kill him, maybe I could set fire to his barn when he's inside it.

No one used 'our place' since our last time. We burned those pictures that he took pretending she's his 'model,' in other words another excuse for him to get her naked. He's such a phony. All he ever paints are boring silos! He has <u>no talent</u>. He couldn't draw her if his life depended on it!!!

I gave Nan my only copy of Anaïs Nin to keep (I can always get another one!) & we both cried when we made love. Will this idiotic guilt of mine ever go away? Math test tomorrow!!! (I sure hope she does okay.)

Prozac evolution

George turns Daisy's journal pages, mesmerised. At last she drops the notebook on the couch and stretches. She should limber up, breathe some air. She should find Zoey.

"George and I are going out," Zoey tells Jerry happily, hanging up the phone. "Don't bother waiting up."

"Translated, Jerry sleeps alone tonight?"

"I guess. Maybe."

"What should I say?"

"I don't know. Whatever you feel like saying."

"Okay, then. What I feel like saying is why don't you and George sleep here? There's room for three on the waterbed."

"I don't think so."

"Should I be packing?"

"Only if you want."

"You said you'd tell me if you wanted me to leave."

She giggles. "All I'm doing is going out with a friend. I could be back in half an hour or tomorrow morning." Outside a car door slams and, blowing a kiss to Jerry, she flings her bag across her shoulders. "Gotta run!"

"Wait!" he says and when she turns he presses something white and flat into her hand. "Prairie grass," he says. "Sweetest in the world. I think you could use a toke."

After a silent ride, George parks at Trafalgar and they alight to walk across the park to the waterfront. Overhead the moon hovers like an anxious mother. City lights shimmer through the mist. Without a breeze the ocean seems at rest.

George caresses Zoey's wrist. "Cold?" she asks.

"A little. Jerry sent a joint."

"What a sweetie."

"Yeah. I miss Eli though. I wonder if I'll always be in love with him."

"Probably."

"If he appeared in front of me this very second and told me that he loved me and wanted to spend his life with me, I'd go anywhere with him. That's so dumb. Isn't that dumb? Have you ever known someone you think you'll always love no matter what?"

"Of course."

"Does it ever get any easier?"

"I'm hoping so."

Pensively Zoey rubs the reefer between her fingers and her thumb. "Why do we always fall for people who are no good for us?"

George leans against the chain-link fence that separates the land from water. "You want me to light that for you? You'll make it disappear if you keep on shredding it."

Zoey thumbs the purple lighter that she bought in Roseville the day she ran into Lori. "Use this," she says and then waits for George to exhale. "Okay, now that you've had time to think, what's your answer?"

"Maybe it's perversity of human nature. A flaw that evolution hasn't mastered yet."

"You know what I think about evolution? I have a theory."

"Here, smoke the rest of this and tell me your theory."

Zoey takes a long slow drag. "I think," she says, "that humans will evolve into having no emotion. It's my Prozac Evolution Theory. We'll all be zombies and not give a shit about each other. It's already started. People meet each other, fuck, marry and divorce in less time than it takes for one baby to be born. They don't even try to make it last, they just give up when they find out the person they're with isn't absolutely perfect. In the olden days, people died of broken hearts but when's the last time you heard of that? Fuck them and move on is all there is. Jean Paul calls it grazing. It's like a great big human garbage dump out there and no one even gives a shit. Humans are supposed to be so special because we can love, but why do the people who don't act with love have all the power?"

"What a pessimist you are!" George laughs. "I've never heard you talk so much!"

"It's probably the humidity. I'm used to drier air." Zoey inhales once more, holding the smoke inside for a long moment. "Or maybe it's this Manitoba grass. Anyway, I think that what they call sociopathy is the whole goal of evolution. For everyone to be like Eli and make decisions from their heads and not their hearts."

"But you said Eli will stay married to Lori all his life," George says.

"That doesn't mean he loves her," Zoey retorts. "He'll do it because he is supposed to have a wife. But he'll always have another bimbo on the side. None of it has anything to do with love."

George shakes her head. "Is that the reason you don't have friends? Because you think emotion is passé and the human race is doomed?"

Zoey butts the roach against the fence. "I don't remember deciding to not have friends, it just didn't happen. I was eight when we moved and by that time the kids in Roseville had already formed their cliques. Besides, I did not fit in, my mom had a job and there was no dad. But if you think it through, there doesn't seem much point to friends. All they are is mirrors. If you're gay you hang with other gays, if you're into sports you hang with jocks, if you're a writer you chum with other writers . . . People hang with other people who are exactly like themselves."

"It's natural to want to be with like-minded people. Have you ever thought that maybe the emotional evolutionary objective, if there is one, is learning to love more instead of less?"

"Then why do the people who don't care for anyone except themselves have all the money and the power? Like, let's say, Nancy. Or Eli."

"Maybe it was only us they couldn't love."

"Do you really think that sadist loved anyone?"

"I think she loved her father, for what it's worth."

"That was sick. I meant real love."

"Sick or not, who's to say it wasn't love? Who gets to define what 'true love' is? You?"

Zoey shivers. "Don't bite my head off, it's just my stupid little theory. Maybe it's wrong. I don't claim to be a rocket scientist. I've been thinking about this stuff, that's all. But you know what? I think we should do something sweet for Jerry."

"I agree. But what? And why?"

"Because he's still unevolved enough to think that he's in love with me. Because he shared his reefer with us. Because smoking pot makes me horny." Zoey giggles. "And what he'd really like has to do with you and me. It's something we can give him easily. Plus it might be fun."

something sweet

They tiptoe into the house as quiet as two guilty mice, then down the darkened stairs. "You should light a candle," whispers George. "So we can see. Maybe he isn't even here."

"I hear him breathing," Zoey whispers back. "But I'll light one anyway." She creates a flame and before she can turn around George is tugging briskly at her clothes. Fabric drops upon the floor until she's standing shivering, her naked nipples taut.

George propels her down onto the bed and in a minute joins her, pressing pelvis against her back and touching her all over with flat exploring hands. Skimming puffy vulva lips, she makes greedy little slurping noises. Zoey groans and squeezes tight her thighs.

Jerry mumbles something restless in his sleep. His eyelids open. "Hiya," he says sleepily. "I thought you weren't coming home tonight."

"You did say this bed is big enough for three."

"Hi there," George says peeking at him over Zoey's shoulder and Zoey kicks the blanket down so he can see what her hands are doing.

"Ahhh," says Jerry. "So it's you." Humming softly he lifts his head onto his palm. His cock kisses Zoey's wrist. "What a sweet surprise," he says happily.

George stuffs her tongue in Zoey's mouth from behind and Jerry sees her nipples stiffen, sees George pry apart her thighs, lift one leg over, rub her cunt against her hip.

"You're the best, Georgie," Zoey whimpers.

Jerry tucks his prick inside his fist. His breath comes quickly from his chest, slides across his tongue and out through his thick lips. George rises up above and spreads her labia with three fingers. Her hard nipples graze his skin and she clamps her hand around his cock, stretching it between Zoey's thigh and her own grinding pelvis. He nibbles Zoey's earlobe, he rubs George's tits. Three tongues touching and his prick is fat and full to bursting between two pussies fucking. He thrusts his fingers in wherever they will fit but then, much too soon, he jerks and spits as everything is punched out of him.

George nudges him away so she can get back to really fucking. "Boys!" she mutters, pinching Zoey's vulva lips together and shaking them as though they were a scruff. With her tongue she urges clit, then nips it with her teeth while she inserts her index finger through the sweaty layers of her cunt. Without urging, Zoey rolls over on her belly and then she strains and gasps and mews while George raps her bum with one flat hand.

"I'm going for a smoke," Jerry mumbles. Not that anyone can hear him. He tugs on his jeans, quickly grabs his shirt and cigarettes and stumbles up the stairs. It's quiet as death up there. He eases the patio door open and steps outside, bracing himself against the September breeze. Below him water splashes against rock. Anchored liners sitting silent with everyone inside asleep. It will be raining in a second, he can smell it.

Anytime he starts to have a little fun something happens, every fucking time. Angrily he smokes his cigarette, wanting something stronger to ease the sinking in his belly. Fuck, fuck, fuck! Nothing ever works out the way it should for him, not even in this fantasy come true. With Eli out of the picture after all these years, it should be simple. But then along comes someone like George to take over and ruin any chance he might have had. It's his fucking turn! He flicks his smoke onto the rocks. Jerry helps himself to Jean Paul's whiskey. He gave Zoey his last reefer; now he'll have to find a place to score.

another pregnancy

Jean Paul is in his kitchen cooking up a feast. "Mmmm," Zoey sings, lifting up a lid. "It smells fantastic! Are we celebrating something?"

He taps her hand with the flat side of his spoon. "Don't peek!" he scolds. "It could do irrevocable damage. Don't you know anything about the distinguished art of cookery?"

Zoey pirouettes around the stove just beyond his reach. "Not a blessed bloody thing!" she coos. "Isn't that just fabulous?"

"What are you so pleased about?"

"Oh, nothing!" she warbles. "Well there is something, but I'm not telling. Where's George?"

"With Jerry. On the balcony."

Zoey bounces through the doorway and pounces upon him. "I've got a secret!" she chants in a kindergarten sing-song voice.

"Stop it!" complains Jerry, grinning. "George, help! Get her off!"

"Georgie!" Zoey whoops, squirming onto her lap. "Gimme tongue! I want lots and lots of tongue."

"Did Smitty put you on Prozac?" George asks suspiciously.

Zoey rolls off, snorting. "Like I need it!"

"Why are you so hyper then?" Jerry asks.

"I've got a really big surprise!" she shouts. "A really great surprise!"

George frowns. "Are you going to let us in on it?"

Zoey hugs herself. "Not yet. Maybe after we've eaten. After this feast JP's been making. I want you all to hear it at the exact same time."

"Dinner's on," Jean Paul calls from the kitchen. "You three wash up."

"What's with you and him?" Zoey whispers loudly. "Have you two made up?"

George shakes her head. "We're trying to be friends again."

"He's way too old for you."

"We're practically the same age."

"Well he acts a lot older."

Tapers tucked into a silver candelabra light the gleaming table. Jean Paul serves and takes his chair. He lifts his goblet. "To friendship," he says.

"Wait!" says Zoey, standing. "Don't drink it yet. I have something to tell you all."

Jerry kicks George's ankle. "Here it comes," he says. "The big announcement."

George holds her glass and looks expectantly at Zoey.

"I just saw Doctor Smitty," she says, then stops. Slowly she looks around the table.

Jerry wriggles with impatience. "Go on! We're listening!"

She lifts her glass with an unsteady hand. "I think I just might cry." Loudly she inhales. "Okay, here goes! Smitty had some news for me. She said . . ."

"What?" asks George impatiently.

"I'm going to have a baby!" Zoey shouts. "She says I'm pregnant!" Her voice grows soft. "I'm pregnant and everything will be okay this time. Smitty promised to take care of me." Then suddenly deflated, she drops onto her chair. For a moment there is silence. Then George leaps up and throws her arms around her. Next Jerry's hugging her and then Jean Paul joins in. Everyone talks excitedly all at once.

"Oh sweetie, I'm so happy for you!" sings George.

"That's great!" Jerry gushes.

"Magnificent!" booms Jean Paul.

Their voices flow around and melt together inside her head and then everything goes spackled silver. Her mouth fills up with bile. "I'm going to be sick," she groans. She staggers down the hallway with George swift upon her heels and crouches by the toilet, retching. "Good thing I haven't eaten yet," she says weakly. "There's nothing to throw up."

George wets a washcloth. "Wipe your face," she says briskly. "We're about to have a celebration."

During dinner Jerry's eyes pan furtively across her time and time again. Jean Paul's heartiness seems a little forced but the food is delicious, the wine is perfect and coffee is served at exactly the right moment. After polite post-meal banter George excuses herself to get back to her manuscript and Jerry asks Zoey for a walk.

The tide is low so they don't need the path. Occasional dogs race past them and seashells crunch beneath their shoes. "So," says Jerry finally. "What got into you? You got so quiet."

"I'm just tired. Nothing's wrong."

"I guess you know why I've been quiet," he offers.

She shrugs. "I didn't really notice."

"What I want to know is whose baby is it?"

"It's mine," says Zoey.

"You know what I mean."

"What difference does it make?"

He clears his throat. "Is it mine?"

"No."

Raindrops on his lashes shiver. "Then whose?"

"Look," says Zoey. "I'm the one who's carrying her. I'll be giving birth to her and taking care of her and raising her. She's mine!"

"In other words, you don't know who the father is."

"You're absolutely right! I haven't got one fucking clue. It could easily be any of the thousand guys I've fucked. Jesus! I didn't think you'd be a prick about it."

"Don't be like that! I'm asking a normal question and I think I have a right to a normal answer, especially considering it could be mine."

Zoey turns away. She looks across the bay. Through the drizzle the dancing North Shore lights flicker like an enormous blinking Christmas ornament. "You just answered your own question," she says. "It might be yours."

"Who else's might it be?" he persists.

"The only thing I know for sure is it can't be George's," she snaps. "Now get off my back, okay?"

"So it could be me or Eli or Jean Paul?"

"That about covers it."

"It's way too perfect here." His voice is rough. "Really. Much too perfect. A person could get lost in it."

"Are you trying to tell me something?"

"I think I'm ready to move on."

"Because I'm pregnant?"

"No, not that. It's just that you seem so solid. I expected something different. I don't know what, just different."

"Maybe you expected weakness."

"I don't think so," he says slowly. "I don't think I want you to be weak. It's more than that; you don't need me. You're like this modern woman, you don't need anyone. You take what you can get and fuck the rest."

"You're so old-fashioned."

"Maybe."

"You want everything defined. You want a father, a mother and a baby. You want everything in its proper place. But real life isn't like that, at least not for me. Look what happened the last time I tried to rely on someone. I've got a second chance and I won't fuck it up. I won't be ashamed, I won't hide or apologise to you or anyone. I have to do this my way. I want to be responsible and if that means being alone forever, that's okay. I'm used to that. I've been in training all my life."

Jerry sighs. "Okay, you made your point and I'll accept it. But I'd like to see the baby sometimes. Send her presents and maybe visit. Could I do that?"

"Of course."

"Will you tell Eli?"

"No," says Zoey. "Absolutely not! He has no right to know."

"Okay."

"And don't you tell him either!"

"I won't."

"Promise?"

"Promise."

"Good."

"You know I love you, Zoey."

"I know. You want to walk some more or go back to the house?"

"Walk," says Jerry gruffly. "I want an evening to remember."

Daisy's Journal

I'm really steamed!! Today I told 'Daddy' what I think about the way he treats his daughter. He was at the museum selling his lousy paintings as part of July 1st holiday bullshit (like anybody gives a crap about his fucking silos!) and Nan had to work. She's supposed to be calling people over, basically pimping him. She's so pretty people want to follow her so he uses her for that. Of course she isn't getting paid for it, unless you count the two inches in his pants as pay. So I went over there to keep her company after I got off shift at the Dairy Queen & the next thing I hear he's hollering at her so loud the whole world can hear. He called her a 'lazy slut' and 'two-bit whore' and he said her 'cunt friends' were scaring off his customers, as if he had any. Dumb fuck. Then she started crying which totally pissed me off. I mean who does he think he is???? Don't answer that. Anyway I got so mad I lost control. I called him a fucking asshole to his face!!!! (I thought he was gonna have a heart attack! It was great!!!) But I guess I went too far. I told him I know everything & then I threatened to tell the cops. To make a long story short, he had security turf me out. I've phoned a million times but he keeps hanging up on me & now I'm really scared about what he'll do to Nan because now he knows she told his dirty little secret. That someone, namely me, knows about the sicko stuff he makes her do. Anyway now she's probably mad at me too and I can't even talk to her to explain my side. I just hope she's still alive because I can't go on living in this disgusting world without her . . . Please, please, please let her be okay!!!!!

July 1st

I don't know what to say. Well I do know what to say but I don't know how to say it. I'm all fucked-up inside. Partly ecstatic and partly terrified. Last night Mr. Rider hanged himself in his barn. Nan found him there this morning. They were supposed to leave for the museum at 9 o'clock and when he didn't show she went to look for him in his studio and there he was. Can you imagine??? I haven't talked to her but I hope she won't blame me for it because of what happened yesterday. She always says she loves him and that she needs him. Now what???? I guess there'll be a funeral. And I know it's bad to think this but I'm glad he's dead. Now maybe she can get some peace for once.

July 16th

Do people really die of broken hearts? Because if they
do ... Nan is gone and she says she's never coming
back. I gave her all my savings for bus fare to
Vancouver. She was going to hitchhike & I couldn't let
her do that. She wouldn't even let me touch her, not
even to kiss her good-bye, she was all fucked up. I can
hardly see this paper because of all the tears pouring
from my eyes. Fuck! Fuck, fuck, fuck, fuck, fuck, fuck!

more questions

Zoey is in George's living room helping her sort and collate. On the floor she sits flipping paper carefully. "There's this thing I've been wondering," she says. "Can I ask you something?"

"Shoot," says George absently from her computer perch.

Zoey pauses, examining the black-and-white photo in her hand. A woman who wears a mask lifts a paddle above another woman who is lying on her belly. She holds the picture up. "It's like this," she says. "I know it's supposed to be twisted, but it kind of makes me feel . . . oh jeez, it's so weird to be saying this aloud to somebody."

George looks at Zoey, then glances idly at the photograph. "What?"

"Hot, I guess," says Zoey. "I mean sometimes I just feel like getting spanked. Is that horrible? Does it mean I'm as warped as her?"

"No," answers George quickly. "Absolutely not. A lot of people get off on it."

"According to what I've been seeing lately, a lot of people are into torture too but I don't think that makes it normal."

George laughs. "By now you should have figured out there's no such thing as normal. It's a long long path from finding the odd spanking sexy to the sort of brutality she was into." She lowers her head once more to her work.

Zoey hesitates. "Did you ever do it?" she asks, flapping the photograph. "I mean this kind of stuff. With Nancy."

For a moment George is silent. "A little," she says finally. "But I draw the line."

"Where do you draw it?" persists Zoey.

"At anything involving blood," says George. "It's not that I think it's evil, I just can't go there. It isn't in my nature."

"How do you know?"

"Because I tried it and it didn't work for me. But Nancy needed it. I mean she really needed it. It was the only way she could get off. That's why our relationship was doomed to fail. She had to meet those needs."

"Did you ever spank anyone?"

"Yes."

"Did you like doing it?"

"Yes," says George.

"Have you had it done to you?"

"What is this? An inquisition?"

"Jeez!" says Zoey. "I thought that you'd be different. Anyone I ever ask about this stuff goes weird on me. I just want to know, without the bullshit."

"I'm sorry," George says. "You're right. Yes, me and Nancy did it to each other. I've done it with other people too."

"Did it turn you on?" Zoey asks. "Because when we were fucking with Jer the other night, you slapped me and I really liked it. Jerry did it too, one time, but when I asked him to do it again he said it meant I wanted to be punished and he refused. I couldn't get him to understand I just liked the way it felt."

"It isn't sick," says George.

"Smitty says this eating disorder thing of mine is all about control. So if I have that, who's to say I don't have some other kinds of problems too? Maybe wanting to be spanked is like a future junkie starting out on pot. Maybe I'll get worse and worse until I'm just like Nancy was, hurting little kids for kicks."

"I'm no expert, but I do know that not every pothead becomes a junkie."

"Would you spank me sometime? If you knew I wanted it?"

"It would be my pleasure. And now, if it's not too much to ask, I need to get to work."

postcard, unsent

august 1

hey daisy!

this is a quick note to tell you I'm doing fine out here & not to worry. I've arrived! I've met some people & I've found a gig modeling. it's easy & it pays quite well. sometime in the next few weeks I should be able to send you back the money that you loaned me for my fare. the problem? - I miss you, a lot! (but that's another story isn't it?) I'm sorry I can't give you an address yet cuz I'm kind of in-between places. so anyway, take care & thanks for everything. I mean that. <u>everything!</u> be sweet! & please don't forget me.

forever nan

consent

"Zoey!" barks George. "My office! Now!" Then shifting back in her chair, she waits.

"Did you call?" Zoey stands in the doorway.

"Yes! Yes I did. Come in. Close the door behind you."

Zoey enters, shuts the door and sits while her boss looks her over critically, red high heels tapping on the hardwood floor.

"On second thought," she says, "I think I want you over here."

Zoey rises. Carefully she walks around the edge of the desk and stands still, her crotch eye-level to George.

"Closer." George pats her knees, noticing how this girl has turned into a woman right before her eyes.

Zoey steps forward. Her tongue feels thick. Nervously she licks her lips with it. "Is this alright?"

"I have a surprise for you. I think you'll like it. But before you can get it, you have to remove your shorts."

With thumping heart, Zoey picks at her belt. She opens the brass buckle and lets the two ends drop.

George snaps her fingers. "Take it out and give it to me."

Zoey slides thick leather slowly from its loops and, with hands trembling, sets it on her boss's outstretched hand. She winces when metal clangs against the desk.

"Now your shorts." George's voice is crisp.

Zoey has been gaining weight so her shorts don't slide easily down her hips. She is forced to lean forward and push them to her ankles. Impatiently George kicks them aside. When Zoey straightens out, her shirt-tail flaps down to cover her naked thighs.

ɔrge tugs at it. "Here. Hold this," she says, forcing pinstriped fabric Zoey's hand.

ʌoey clutches it against her belly. Cool air fans her skin turning pores to goosebumps. Then George pushes her mouth roughly against the mound of rusty pubic fur set before her like a banquet. She probes the vulva lips apart with sharp red nails while her other hand works shirt buttons until two round breasts pop out.

"Your tits are getting bigger," George says, handling them, "now that you are pregnant. I think it's very sexy, this new you."

Breathing through her teeth, Zoey clenches every muscle in her body while George's knuckles twist her heavy nipples. The belt lies upon the desk. Through the window Zoey sees a neighbour lift a sack of trash into his bin. He glances up and she wonders if he's seen her standing here being humiliated, getting slowly naked.

"I think you will enjoy what's coming," says George. "Usually it goes something like this." She turns Zoey to face the desk. Spreading her labia, she presses it against the ridge. Zoey stays quite still where she is placed, barely breathing. Now George lifts the belt, winding it several times around her hand. "Do you know what I'm doing?" she asks softly and Zoey nods. "And you're sure you want me to?" Zoey nods again. "Then bend over." Zoey leans across the desk while George rubs her buttocks with the hand that holds the leather. "You deserve a good spanking," she says hoarsely.

Zoey wriggles against the desk to make her fat clit throb. She is rigid with desire, tingles from her cunt are racing through her body, her lips are thick and she wants someone to bite them hard. Since George is busy elsewhere, she sucks on them herself until she swallows blood. Every time George strikes her bum, Zoey's pussy jams against the wood. Between the spanking she is giving her, George pokes things into her, trading fingers for a pencil for the handle of a hairbrush, probing all of Zoey's burning holes till she is on fire, throbbing head to toe. And all she wants is more and more of everything that's being done to her.

"Turn around," George orders.

Zoey obeys, thrusting out her pelvis, eager for the tangy bite of leather. Time and time again it nips into her snatch where she is swollen stiff and dripping. Then George leans down. Removes a red high heel. Raising it, she sits up straight and Zoey groans. Slowly George brings the sharp heel forward. Teases clit with it, rolling it around in gentle circles, then harder, firmer, up and down until at last she grinds it into Zoey's aching greedy cunt. "That's it!" she pants. "You can let go! Let go *now!*" And Zoey does, whimpering while her steamy cream drenches George's hand. Then she begins to cry. As though her heart is shattering. And she falls exhausted into welcome outstretched arms. "There, there," soothes George, gently patting shoulders. "*Now* you have what you deserve."

luck

George's publisher has rushed the book to print. Nancy's house has been smudged clean and it's up for sale. No one has found her killer yet but George and Zoë have planned a raffle of her sleazy clothes. They intend to use the money to start a fund for kids who've been abused. Jerry is backpacking across Europe to find his roots and has been mailing postcards to gush about his new surroundings. Jean Paul is alternately sweet and sullen; he still wants George to be his wife and now he thinks he'd like to father Zoë's baby too.

They are having brunch in George's kitchen when the book arrives, beautifully bound, glossy and sweet-smelling. Zoë pores over George's shoulder until she pulls away annoyed. "Get your own copy," she scolds. "There's nineteen more of them in that box."

"I want to look at it with you," says Zoë stubbornly. "Otherwise we'll be on different pages and I won't know what you're going on about. Where is my name? You said it would be here."

George points. "Here it is, in 'special thanks.'"

"Good! They got the new spelling. Zoë looks so much more sophisticated than Zoey, don't you think?"

"I think they did a lovely job."

"I don't know what I'd rather do right now," says Zoë. "This is so exciting and I feel so edgy. I kind of feel like going out and I also sort of feel like having you eat me and I'd like to go for a walk except it's raining out as usual. We've worked so hard for this and finally it's here. I can't believe we're actually holding it in our very hands!"

"Someday my sweet, your name will be on a cover. Zoë, all by its lonesome, and you'll be a famous poet and I'll be so proud! I'll say *I knew you when* and I'll order you an ocean of champagne and a trillion roses in celebration."

Zoë giggles. "By then I'll have a toddler too. And don't forget about the handsome henchmen! I want those henchmen!"

"Of course, handsome henchmen! At your every beck and call."

"Absolutely."

"And in the meantime . . ."

"Yes?"

George drops the book. "You just have me. I say let's go to bed and fuck and then we'll nap and wake up sexy. And then I'll take you out to dinner, all expenses paid."

"Okay," says Zoë happily. "You talked me into it. Lead the way!"

"Oh! Wait!" says George, stopping suddenly in mid-step. "There's something I forgot."

"What's that?"

"We have to take Nancy's book to bed with us. For luck."

"Ah yes!" Zoë grins. "More luck is precisely what we need."

The End

*I extend my deep appreciation to Colin Smith and Audrey McClellan
for their practical assistance and enthusiasm,
and my gratitude to Chris Petty and Patrick Friesen
for their encouragement and grace.*

Special thanks to the BC Arts Council for funding a portion of this work.